WINNER OF THE 30TH ANNUAL
INTERNATIONAL 3-DAY NOVEL CONTEST

IN THE GARDEN OF MEN

JOHN KUPFERSCHMIDT

3-Day Books Vancouver Toronto

Cover and Interior Design
Jane Lightle, Bibelot Communications Ltd.

Cover Photo by Allan Brown

Library and Archives Canada Cataloguing in Publication

Kupferschmidt, John, 1983-
In the garden of men / John Kupferschmidt.

ISBN 978-1-55152-239-5

I. Title.
PS8621.U64I5 2008 C813'.6 C2008-902613-6

Distributed in Canada by Jaguar and in the United States by Consortium through Arsenal Pulp Press (www.arsenalpulp.com).

Published by
3-Day Books
341 Water Street, Suite 200
Vancouver, B.C., V6B 1B8, Canada

www.3daynovel.com

Printed in Canada by Friesens

ENVIRONMENTAL BENEFITS STATEMENT

3 Day Novel Contest (The) saved the following resources by printing the pages of this book on chlorine free paper made with 100% post-consumer waste.

TREES	WATER	ENERGY	SOLID WASTE	GREENHOUSE GASES
4	1,348	3	173	325
FULLY GROWN	GALLONS	MILLION BTUs	POUNDS	POUNDS

Calculations based on research by Environmental Defense and the Paper Task Force. Manufactured at Friesens Corporation

To the men and women who send their laughter to break walls of oppression and combat injustice. To those who speak truth when we do not want to hear, show us what we choose not to see, and urge us to act when comfort numbs us to what must be done. To you, we owe our freedom.

PART ONE

I do not believe in goodness. Undoubtedly there are good things in life: a day in the sun; a pint of beer; a freshly opened package of cigarettes; poetry, even in all its banality and indulgence; certain aspects of women; the music of Beethoven and Dvořak; lying in bed, cigarette in hand, staring out from my flat on the top floor of my building and looking at Prague with all its steeples and towers; a walk along the river at dusk when the city is set aflame with an auburn and orange tinge from the day's dying sun. In my estimation, all these are good things, but they are of my own creation; they are not universally good. My experience with Beethoven is different than yours; perhaps you prefer the swing of Glenn Miller, or perhaps your arthritis makes walking in the dampness along the flowing Vltavá detestable. There is no such thing as universal good, and this is why I say that I do not believe in goodness.

In Czechoslovakia, as in every state, goodness has been heralded by one conqueror after another, each as oppressive as his predecessor. As the powerful rise like a faithful and lethal tide on a nation's shores, as sure as time, as sure as greed, as sure as vice, goodness is claimed by the powerful to subdue the powerless. This is why I despise Petr Ludek. He believes in goodness. He is goodness in all its childish stupidity. In 1938 he stood in Wenceslas Square and sang our anthem in stubborn defiance as Hitler and the Nazi Party ascended the presidential palace. Because Petr thought himself good, they killed him. In 1948 Petr Ludek danced in the streets, propelled by the illusion of a future where all men were equal, as the Communist Party took power and promised eternal happiness for the people. Five years later, Petr Ludek found himself locked in a cell for indicting a state that murdered its own people and made new masters from the moulds of old ones. And a few months ago he once again took his fiancée, Zdeňa Havlová, by the hand, and joined the rest of the people of Prague in a dancing stupor as Alexander Dubček rose to the presidential palace and declared a new future for us all. Less than eight months later, on the night of August 20, 1968, the Soviet Union and its Warsaw Pact allies sent four hundred thousand troops and six thousand tanks to occupy us and secure the state of Czechoslovakia "for the people." This, despite the fact that it was "the people" who had danced in the streets at Dubček's rise, and it was "the people" who refused the bribes of rations and aid, and in protest spat in the faces of the new conqueror. Yes, "the people" have been a convenient accomplice throughout history. I doubt I will ever meet them. And now, as the Russians come, Petr Ludek once again finds himself hunted and made to disappear. And though it has happened to him countless times before, he is surprised and cries out injustice. Petr Ludek is the virtuous agitator of history; he assails and decries and, beyond all reason, holds onto a vision of the world full of goodness and tenderness. Yet his life is a testament to the contrary.

The World Continues on August 21, 1968

On the morning of August 21, 1968, the people of Czechoslovakia woke to find themselves occupied by the Soviet Union. Our president had been arrested and taken to Moscow in the middle of the night, and a massive campaign to purge the nation of counter-revolutionaries had begun. I woke and found I had been promoted. By education I was a lawyer, by occupation I was a Party bureaucrat. Before August 21, I had held a small desk at the Housing Ministry passing papers and filling out forms. There are, unsurprisingly, few opportunities for a lawyer under a dictatorship. It was not an exciting position, but I had never sought excitement or adventure and was left alone with few expectations made of me. But after August 21, I was moved to my own closed-room office with my very own grimacing secretary, Jitka Navratilová. The Soviets had mistaken my apathy to the world as antipathy towards Dubček and his allies, and as fidelity to the Party. I had thought of it as a fortunate misunderstanding and did not see any need to correct it.

With Dubček had come spring and the streets began to blossom with Petr Ludeks and Zdeňa Havlovás. Dancing throngs made buildings dizzy and the Russians tremble. I did not dance. I am not Petr Ludek, nor do I wish to be. I sat by my window and looked out onto this city that danced and laughed and celebrated and believed it had found its salvation. They danced in a whirl like white cherubs, just as innocent and pure, just as naïve and lost. Do not mistake me for a Communist; I am ambivalent and find my opinion inconsequential. One ideology is as good as the next. One prescription does not sit above another and, even if it did, power does not listen to the will of the people (despite its fervent rhetoric). So tell me Petr Ludek, what is the point? In his answer, he will spout the conventional wisdom of his peers. He may invoke poetry and regale me with the intrinsic beauties of a flower, or the sacrifice that comes from the love of a mother for her children. But a flower is just a flower, and a mother's love for her children, while beautiful in a way, is still full of vanity, a possessive love to reclaim youth. He will say, "Tell me then, what is the alternative: despair?" No. Despair occurs when you hope and then realize that your hope is unattainable. What I feel is indifference. The world is neither good nor bad, only caught in the sad realities of our flawed creation. Goodness does not belong in the streets and the world of men, only with angels and children.

A few days after the Soviet invasion, the crowds had for the most part dispersed, but still there remained a dedicated throng that patrolled the streets with chants of liberty, freedom, and democracy. No doubt every individual's name had been recorded and put on some list where they were joined by the names of other undesirables. I was returning from being introduced to my new office and was unsuccessfully navigating around these shouting cherubs. I hoped to remain insignificant to anyone that might glance at me; a man in a grey suit who made his way through this tide of history with his head down and hastening feet. With my eyes fixed on the cobblestones, I took note of legs and feet. They stood in every manner of pant and skirt, shoe and sandal. Neatly hemmed trousers clashed with frayed bell bottoms and bleached jeans; worn leather sandals mingled with heels and polished loafers.

A thunderous roar overwhelmed the street and the cries of my countrymen rose to create a terrible symphony. I looked up to see tanks rolling into the crowd at the far end of the street. Fists shot into the air and chants ballooned around the Soviet soldiers who marched in line and flanked the rumbling tanks—a flagrant parade of power that with each step sealed Czechoslovakia's fate in the annals of history.

I looked back to the ground and moved quickly. If anything were to happen, if I were to be found among these misguided, no questions would be asked, no investigation made. Only a signed warrant and a cell would greet me. My pace quickened and adrenaline bid my feet to run. But as the street came to a slight incline I stood still, and found myself able to look ahead at the stirring crowd. It melted into one unified mass of righteousness, and stretched forth into a fantastical moving beast, with a thousand arms raised in defiance and voicing one harmonious cry for justice. Into this monster penetrated the line of Soviet soldiers and tanks. The juxtaposition made the indomitable masses appear impotent and their raised fists and angry cries changed from a display of power to something entirely pathetic and childish. The synchronized march of the soldiers, the rumble of tanks and the angry cry of Prague's citizenry shook the ground, releasing a thin veil of dust over the street and its mad inhabitants, coating the righteous and unrighteous alike. People brushed past me, pushing forward to reach the front lines, and despite my apprehensions I found myself standing still, watching the unfolding history before me.

And there in the distance, not far from the incline where I watched, walked Anežka, veiled by the curtain of dust and noise, her bright emerald-green shawl a shot of colour in the crowd. She was about fifty metres away, but I could clearly make out her features and indomitable stride. Occasionally she stopped and looked about her with a curious smile of amusement, watching the scene as if it were the climax of an opera whose story had been reworked until it no longer held any message. I watched her to see if she raised her hand or voice at the rumbling tanks and marching soldiers, but she never did. She only stood to the side, content to watch the opera from a distance. It was as though the two of us had prestige tickets to the season's most epic production, where the misguided battled with one another over the ownership of righteousness.

A small band of young men ran past, pushing me aside in their excitement to reach the front lines of this insufferable carnival. I stepped forward to steady myself but the shoving proved too much for my briefcase and papers burst from it, littering the cobblestones. I dove to rescue them before they fell prey to the trampling angels, grabbing frantically between legs and feet. When all had been retrieved I looked up. The tanks were nearing me and their roar set the buildings to tremble. I looked through the crowd to find the emerald shawl, but I could not see it and cursed the reckless boys who had spilled my briefcase. I was disappointed that the moment of mutual curiosity that Anežka and I shared had been so short-lived. It pleased me to know that there were sensible people in this world and that I occasionally shared my bed with one of them—even if I might pay her to be there.

For fear of being crushed to the walls by angels and devils alike, I slipped into an alley and waited for the tanks and crowds to diminish. A little over an hour later I slipped back into the street that remained fertile with Petr Ludeks and Zdeňa Havlovás and with my eyes on the cobblestones I launched into a brisk walk towards my flat.

The First List

I live down Prokopskă Street, just across the courtyard from where a frowning bust of Lenin sits with the accusing eyes of a conqueror. Before Lenin, there sat a glaring bust of Stalin; before Stalin was a pensive Masaryk, the great Liberator of the First Czechoslovak Republic. And before that, Zdislava Berková, patron saint of difficult marriages and people ridiculed for their piety, kept vigilant eyes on the courtyard. In Prague, time is measured by the busts of men who rise and fall with their regimes. In my life I have seen the Germans replaced by the Russians, by the Communists, then the Socialists, and now the Soviets. Like the bust sitting quietly in the middle of the courtyard, I have sat quietly and watched the oppressed become conquerors, and conquerors become oppressors. That is the way of things here, and those who weep or dance as oppressors change clothes are the children of angels who do not understand the world that man has created.

I soon discovered that my predecessor had disappeared on the night of August 20. When I asked Jitka for an explanation, she scowled and said he just "hadn't come back to the office," and without further discussion she continued filing a stack of papers on her desk. I did not ask again. I knew better than to delve further into such a precarious subject. These days, people disappear without a whisper of memory. Fear can obliterate a lifetime of camaraderie when an accusing eye falls on your back. A dreariness has fallen over Prague as lists grow longer and people disappear quicker, quieter.

The first time I came upon such a list was the day after my birthday. I had spent the night before drinking alone in my apartment, staring out onto the city. The following morning, as I stepped, hung over, into my office, I had no thought of anything but the drill that bore into my head. On my way in, I grunted a greeting to Jitka, who courteously replied with a disapproving grimace. I closed the door behind me, relieved to be hidden from the world, and staggered over to the window to pull down the blind against the assaulting sun. When I turned to my desk I saw a pile of papers. Upon closer examination I realized it was a list of names. Row upon row of names, listed in columns of Age, Occupation, Address, Name(s) of Child(ren), Spouse, and Offence. In this last category, the most common were "engaged in counter-revolutionary activities" and, more poetically, "traitor to the will of the people." Beside the list was a stack of empty warrants. These needed to be filled in from the information on the list and then signed by the Justice Ministry. That is, signed by me.

I began the task with little thought other than to complete it and spent the day filling out each warrant with as much diligence and accuracy as I could muster after a night of heavy drinking. It was only when the time came to sign them that a curious hesitation came over me and I released the pen and raised my feet and legs to rest on the desk. I lit a cigarette and inhaled deeply, trying to shake off the reluctance in my hands. The blind was still pulled down and it cast a striped pattern of light and shadow against the far wall. As I exhaled, the smoke drifted into the yellow bars of sunlight. I took a long drag and then opened my mouth and let the smoke waft from my lips. Illuminated by the lines of light, it took on the shapes of hills and rivers, masquerade faces and weepy eyes, constellations and continents. I thought of Petr Ludek, his dancing in the street and his diatribes on goodness, and I found myself greatly vexed. You cannot bend the will of an uncompromising power, just as the smoke could not bend the bars of light. I leaned over and put out the cigarette. Then I picked up the pen and signed the warrants.

With the ink still drying on the pages, I gathered them up and walked out of my office to Jitka's desk. For a moment I held them and once again Petr Ludek came into my mind. I saw the police walking up the long staircase to his apartment and knocking on his door. They would present the warrant (signed by me) and ask him to come with them. I wondered what he would do: if he would turn and run, if he would look horrified and beg for absolution, or if they would drag him away while he shouted slogans of freedom and decried the Russians as hypocrites and invaders. But the image that settled and would not drift from me was Petr Ludek quietly taking his hat and coat and stepping out into the hallway with police on either side of him, as lesser officers marched into the apartment to search for incriminating documents that they would undoubtedly find. Jitka peered at me from behind the lenses of her heavy framed glasses. I smiled and placed the papers in front of her. A strange feeling of triumph fell over me. I knew I was not responsible for putting these people away; I was merely a stop on the way, a stop that could easily be skipped. But the thought of these angels being taken away made me glad, and not from the knowledge that the Communist nation was being safeguarded. Rather, my triumph stemmed from a darker place that knew angels did not belong in this world of devils—and wanted them expelled.

As I ate dinner, I thought of those names and little else. Names that by morning tomorrow would disappear, only remaining as quiet memories laced with damning fear. I had not held such antipathy for Petr Ludek and Zdeňa Havlová before today and yet as I thought of them, my hatred for them grew. I was required to hate them and so I did.

I sat in the little restaurant on Svoboda Road staring out at nothing in particular as pedestrians walked by pursuing their evening errands. In Czech, *svoboda* means "freedom," and so I found it curious that the state named streets after the virtues it stole from its subjects. The people walked back and forth, their faces hanging heavy with concern as though the world had shifted and they were having trouble regaining their stride. And I could not help but wonder which of these passers-by were Petrs and which ones Zdeňas. Had I been given the discretion of the Party, I surely would have run out onto the street and called them out. I would make a declaration on the greatness of the Soviet Empire and express the deepest appreciation for the Russian occupation and wait for all the Petr Ludeks and Zdeňa Havlovás in Prague to line up to debate and argue with me. Then I would call the police and have each and every one arrested, have each one made to disappear, have each one forgotten. And as they were taken away I would laugh at their stupidity and their innocence. I would laugh at their misplaced "goodness" until I was left alone in the street with the fearful and sensible and the world would continue to turn without the indulgences of angels.

The people continued to move along the darkening street, wearing their pathetic sadness like umbrellas against the rain of empire. Yet for all my declarations, the reasons for my hatred of Petr Ludek evaded me. To be sure, I found him frustrating in his thoughts and actions, but this was not where my abhorrence for him stemmed. Nor was it because I was a Party faithful and hated his opposition. I did not feel any particular fealty to the Party and rather than despising his opposition, I was baffled by it. I could not understand what cause someone would have to care who it was that rose to the presidential palace. Did it really matter? Suffering continued. People continued to live in misery whether it was a Russian, German, Czech, or Slovak that ran the country. Do not oppose, and you will be spared. Do not condemn and you will live. So I ate my dinner in bewilderment, for I could not understand why Petr·Ludek confronted power when there was no hope of success.

Anežka

After my stomach was full, thoughts of Petr and Zdeňa still plagued me, and so I made my way to the secret lounge on Kaprova Avenue, where I am a frequent visitor. It is here I met Anežka over two years ago, and have found myself returning for the sole purpose of seeing her, more often than I should like to admit. She told me once that she liked me because I did not cry on her shoulder, nor did I beat her. I was pleased she liked me, but found it unfortunate that her criteria for affection should be so low. The declaration was also reflective of our time together, which amounted to little more than the satiation of my lust.

The host brought me to my usual table in the lounge, and I sat waiting to see Anežka, biding my time with brandy and cigarettes. As time went by, I watched as the men around me groped the women of the lounge. The men took on all appearances; young and old, some tall and skinny, others short and fat, and still others lay in the degrees between, but through them all was a common thread of ugliness that in other surroundings might have remained unseen. Despite the illegality of the lounge, most were Party members or those who had quickly and conveniently made allies out of the Russians after the invasion. These were the same people who, before August 21, before the Soviet tanks rolled into Prague, were dancing in the street, holding Petr Ludek by one hand and Zdeňa by the other. But realizing that idealists and moralists have little else but ethics in their pockets, they left Dubček's dancing circles and filed into the ranks of the Communist Party, praying they had enough to pay off anyone who could accuse them of having ever danced in a circle. I watched these animals and their foreplay of vodka and beer, their vacuous ritual before paid sex. I thought of the names and I wondered where Petr Ludek would be now: arrested, in questioning, being beaten? Or perhaps he was still free, still grasping for a dream that had already failed. I thought of him sitting with friends in a crowded apartment, smoke hovering near the ceiling as they drank and laughed. In this place men drank to forget, but Petr and Zdeňa drank to remember. In their laughter they remembered the poetry, the politics, the stories, the ideas they used to hold onto the goodness they think they have found. They talked, laughed and drank to keep alive the emblazoned intellectual; to breathe life into the dead existence of a futile resistance.

As this scene played in my mind, it ignited with the present before my eyes. A blur of visions contrasting as harshly as day and night stood in remarkable parallel. A quiet rage filled me as I imagined Petr and his friends turning red with discussion and debate, Zdeňa and her peers pink with laughter and intellectual argument. It was not from jealousy or resentment that I despised them, but it was the anger and frustration that an adult must feel when a child refuses to acknowledge a truth. When in stubborn defiance a child cries that night cannot fall, and his belief is so strong he will continue to play long after the sun has fallen and the moon has risen. In the light of the moon, the child will dance and yell at his parents that they were wrong because there is still light to play, and so he remains dancing and playing in the light of his own truth. I am the adult, and Petr and Zdeňa are the children. This is not a world of poetry and politics. It is a world of facts. Facts that cannot be changed. Light gives way to night, power gives way to oppression, and man gives way to sin. I took a sip from my brandy and continued to watch the odious men grope the women. At least here sin was recognized, without pretensions of morality. Here we all knew that in us and through us, no salvation could be found.

Lost in my thoughts, I did not notice when Anežka sat down beside me until I felt her hand gently resting on my thigh. I turned to her and she smiled briefly but did not speak. Her face was slightly narrow, though her features were in perfect proportion. She was not fond of rouge or lipstick and rarely wore it, an attribute that had first drawn me to her. Chestnut-brown hair framed her face and fell over her shoulders. It was the same colour as her eyes, whose stare declared a determination of character that made our encounters flow without any moral hesitations. I smiled back at her and we spoke for a few moments of the weather and the coming autumn. It was then I remembered I had seen Anežka at the protest, watching the citizens of Prague clash with empire as a spectator might watch rival teams compete at a football game. I thought it strange that neither of us mentioned the Russians or the demonstrators, but was appreciative for the comfort this silence afforded my over-ponderous brain. I asked if she had any engagements later in the evening. She told me she did not and we rose from the table.

I followed her out of the lounge and down a hallway that led to rooms officially provided so drunk men could sleep off their stupor, but in reality serving as places where men like me paid to quench their loneliness with women like Anežka. We entered her room and she began to undress. I followed suit and soon we were lying on the bed, limbs entangled, lips caressing, hands roaming. There was an ambiguous cold formality that was the norm in our encounters and kept us separate even as we were intimate. I dismissed it as an excusable reality of our circumstances. Here I lay on top of her thrusting. But even now as I fucked her, I could not displace the list of names from my head and I thought about Petr and I wondered whether he had ever paid a woman for sex. He filled my mind, he and Zdeňa both, and as I groped Anežka, I could not help but think that when they made love, Petr and Zdeňa were tender with each other. They would kiss long and deeply, hold each other and flow into each other like two rivers joining and then returning to their own currents. It did not deserve the same name as the animalistic fornications to which I was subjecting Anežka. As I thought of this, the same rage that had come over me in the lounge filled me and I began to thrust harder and harder into Anežka as if to erase the images of Petr and Zdeňa. But the harder I thrust, the more vivid the images became, and anger propelled me until Anežka began a quiet whimper. But I did not stop. As if to prove to this vision that tenderness was implausible, I continued my assault on Anežka until, between the beastly tones of my grunts, all I could hear were her pitiful sounds. The sentimental image of Petr and Zdeňa dissolved, replaced with the cold fuck of my body over Anežka and her woeful tears. Now all that remained was the harsh darkness of our situation; slapping flesh without affection or emotion.

Once I had climaxed, I did not lie down beside her as I normally did, but rose and quickly dressed. Before leaving, I placed some bonds on her nightstand that allowed her to shop at the Bílá Labut, where Western extravagances were made available to the well positioned or well connected. A "gift" for an evening's entertainment. Without a word I stepped into the hallway and walked out of the lounge and into the foggy street. I had claimed victory over Petr and Zdeňa. I had made them vanish. Two dozen such people that I had passed into their fate would disappear tonight. I had made them disappear, their silly tenderness and impossible love. I had erased them from my mind and could claim victory. But as I turned the corner, it was not with the spring of a victor, but with the dragging feet of a man who knows that he has killed some small piece of goodness.

Prague

When I arrived home I did not turn on the lights. I pushed open the large window that looked onto a sweeping vista of the city. Sprawled out before me were the red roofs of buildings, turned into heavy maroon under the moonlight and intermittently eclipsed by the dark shadows of towers and steeples. Prague is the city of a thousand steeples. Of streets that unfold in a maze of alleys and courtyards. Of ornate buildings that stand as testaments to history. Of mournful saints who hover over shop windows and churches alike, openly judging, pitying the throngs that walk the streets below them. They can judge because they are not real. Their hearts do not have to contend with sin. But now in Prague and in most places on this side of the Iron Curtain, it is the Communist Party that glares down upon us. Watching us, accusing us, and chastising us for half-hearted zeal in the proletarian cause. The Party and the saints, they hover above us, reaping the benefits of not walking among us as real men. They are the creators of their perfection and so measure our shortcomings, judge us, and urge us to confess.

I turned from the window and grabbed a bottle of rum and a dirty glass from the counter top. It was cluttered with dirty dishes and empty bottles and had been since well before the invasion. I sat down and poured myself a drink. Looking out onto the city I drank steadily, hoping to keep any thoughts of Petr Ludek or Anežka at bay. Here I sat, drinking and watching the city fall asleep while Anežka lay on her bed, the bonds still sitting on the nightstand. And Petr Ludek, where was he? Hiding from me and my villainy. I circumvented the empty glass and grabbed the bottle. Here I sat as villain. The role had been set for me and so I played the part. I had never had the ambition to be a villain or a hero. Neither goodness nor villainy inspires me. I cannot say that I know what goodness is or where it can be found. If I were good, would I know it? And yet I know that I am not. Nor do I wish to be good. To be good, one must remain a child, hidden away in some vacant Garden of Eden, eyes closed to the world, separate from the realities of man's creation. This is where Petr and Zdeňa live. In the garden of Dubček, in the garden of a future without sin or toil, a garden where we all walk as brother and sister in contented virtue. But there are no such gardens, no such futures. Look closer and in each proclaimed Eden you will find deceit, abhorrence, jealousy, greed, and lust. Look closer and you will find intolerance draped in virtue. Look closer and goodness is revealed as the unconscious neurosis of humanity's collective despair.

I brought the bottle down and ran a hand over my wet lips. They were sticky and for a moment I tasted Anežka. My head dropped to my chest and I rose to stare out upon the city. Fewer windows were illuminated now, and an ominous silence hovered in the air and rode a breeze that smelled of an impending storm. The occasional dog barking or drunkard calling echoed through the air and declared the emptiness of the world. This despair of humanity; why do we hope? We peg our lives on it, clinging to the future for salvation as we kill for the present. Man carries himself today and believes God will carry him tomorrow. But no salvation arrives. History forbids it. There in the folds of time lies the inescapable argument against ourselves, and against our future. There can never be salvation because we cannot remove the innate destruction that belies our nature. A new Party will rise, a new God will condemn us, a new leader extol us, and our hopes for a future without sin will propel us to fail, to destroy, to sin for the moment because the world will be better for it tomorrow.

My head was spinning with rum and thought, with Anežka and Petr Ludek. I dragged myself from the window and stumbled to my bed, keeping the bottle steady in my hand as I lay my head down on the pillow. I could still feel the breeze, and smell the herald of rain. And were my thoughts and feelings not so weighty, I would have floated away upon this kinetic stream of air to a land where there were no men or women. No ideologies or religions. Only the breeze that announced the change of seasons and carried rain and revealed the sun. Away from the hopes and fantasies that deny imperfection and claim to hold salvation. For it is hope and fantasy that exploit our weakness and stupidity, and set one garden against another. Proletariat against Capitalist; Catholic against Protestant; Muslim against Christian; Fascist against Democrat; East against West. Nation is set against Nation because there is never a single fantasy that is universal. We fight. We kill for the vision. We make lists of those to disappear and we banish these unfavourables from our gardens of paradise.

In Prague such visions are brokered by impossible idealists and deceptive bureaucrats; by the faithful and the unfaithful alike. Gardens sowed by the sword, whose wielder looks up into the eyes of the saints and cries out his vision of truth. A truth that is beyond reason and reproach. And in my drunken stupor I could hear their cries to the saints, their declarations of truth proclaimed to the universe. But the saints do not listen; they do not intervene and create a future of paradise. So the day comes when people forget the truth and it no longer seems to be anything but false. And so the crowd dwindles and sword returns to its sheath. Until one day a child picks it up and declares a new truth, and the crowds return and take up arms again and chant in unison to the deaf saints. It seems unknown to even themselves that the crowd is made of up saints; made up of the very creation the masses extol. Here in this city, where the saints hover over you, goodness is as elusive, as intangible as the sinless fantasies of her people.

A Second List

The breeze had deceived me; no rain had come. When I woke the next morning my head was heavy and beside the bed lay a puddle of rum where I had dropped the bottle in my drunkenness. I washed my face and in the act dissolved the last evidence of my evening with Anežka. I swore to the mirror that I would not visit Anežka again for some time. I did not feel shame or embarrassment at what had transpired between us. On the contrary it was a kind of ambiguous uncertainty, which whispered of a woeful and bitter pride. I had taken goodness and hurt it, made it sour. Made it disappear. But should I see Anežka again I would apologize for my barbarism, for I had not meant to hurt her so, and though I did not feel regret, I felt something that closely resembled it.

At the office, I let my thoughts wander as I skimmed over the morning's newspaper. As I sat at my desk, Jitka walked up to me and, greeting me with a curious frown, placed a pile of documents on my desk. Then she turned and walked away without a word. I took the pile of papers and sifted through them. My eyes fell on row upon row of names, column after column of age, occupation, names of children, husbands and wives. The information for a hundred people sat before me. Their future was seemingly written in the pages, their past being unwritten because their fantasy differed from the one with power. Perhaps because their gardens did not include lists just as this one, and bureaucrats like me. I put the papers down and looked out the window. I had never really looked out onto the scene. The view was anything but spectacular, just anonymous grey apartment buildings that huddled together, melting into the city's monotone diorama until they were indistinguishable from one another. And I wondered why these names had not remained indiscernible. What cause would these buildings have to step forward and make themselves noteworthy? What arrogance and self righteousness would be required for such an act? I stayed in the acceptable grey; unexceptional, unidentifiable, unknown, and I spent much of the morning staring out the window, trying to imagine what would cause a man or woman to stand out and declare themselves.

After lunch I took the list in hand and began to fill out the empty warrants with the information contained in the rows and columns of the pages:

Drahoslavová, Ludmilla
D.o.b: May 3, 1944;
62 Beneš Street, Brno;
1 child - Tomas - d.o.b. February 28, 1958
No spouse
2nd Grade Teacher
Counter-revolutionary activities.

And once I had completed the first warrant, I began on the second, then the third. Each one was filled out with greater ease. One warrant, one name. One following another until beside me there amassed a pile of papers, pages that contained the names of those who would disappear. But in order to make the great collective forget its dissidents, I had to remember them. Each name as I typed it became seared into my memory. Each occupation, each child, each address, each spouse, each date of birth melted into my brain and I began to see them. They passed before me indifferently: mothers with their children, young idealists waving their fists in the air, students carrying their fall textbooks, fathers with their sons and daughters, wives linking arms with their husbands.

A curiously temporary existence danced before me, these lives that hung between a grey of life and non-existence. But here none begged me to let them fall into the cracks of bureaucratic error. None looked at me longingly, hiding regret in their eyes. Here in my office, their spirits were evoked as their lives disappeared. A sombre parade of life passed before me as my fingers typed out their sentences and forged their future.

Outside the sky hung heavy with the promise of rain, but still the sidewalks remained dry. As I continued to work from one warrant to the next I could not help but think of the events of the night before. I could not help but think of how I had hurt Anežka, of how I had sent Petr and Zdeňa away. I had resigned their love to the fate of the names before me. I had taken their tenderness and twisted it. I tried to recall their gentle touch, their seemingly silly expression of love. These two figments of my imagination who made love as they lived, passionately and with affection, an antithesis to the realities of the world around them. As my fingers moved faster and faster over the keys, those soft images that I had imagined between Petr and Zdeňa could not be evoked. The faces of the names still stood before me, and they watched me search for that which I had so eagerly killed. But the harder I tried to remember them, the only thing that came to mind were the quiet whimpers of Anežka. I had won. I had made Petr and Zdeňa disappear from my mind. I had forgotten them. And still my cynicism was unsatisfied as I furiously typed away more names that would soon too be removed from history.

Desolation crept over me and I rose from my typewriter and looked out the window. It comforted me to see the buildings, uniform and indiscernible; a grey mass without detail or poignancy. But behind me stood the ghosts of people forgotten, so I grabbed my coat and, declaring to Jitka that I was not feeling well, ran into the street. As rain burst forth from the sky and droplets struck the sidewalk, I broke into a determined stride, careful not to turn or let my eyes move beyond the sidewalk for fear that the shadows of the forgotten were following me.

Who Is Petr Ludek?

For some time now I have been searching for the answer to a particularly elusive question. How does one keep faithful to goodness? There exists an important distinction between this question and the question of what makes a good man, or who is good, or what is good. When one asks how does one keep faithful to goodness, there is a supposition that goodness already exists and it is merely the choice of man to commit himself to it or not. Though I do not believe in goodness, that does not stop others from believing in it. And so I ask, what holds one's belief, without the inducements of religion or ideology? What keeps a man tethered to virtue? The unfortunate approximation of an answer that I have come to is Petr Ludek.

In 1938, Czechoslovakia was offered by her allies to Hitler as a token of Western goodwill. I was a small boy living with my parents in the village of Orlický Hrad. It lies about a hundred miles east of Prague at the foot of the Orlické Mountains, which stretch out to the Polish border in waves of infinite pastures and green valleys. In our village lived a man whose name was Petr Ludek. After almost seven years of Nazi rule, the winter of the German retreat was for many a chance to exact vengeance, but for others a moment to reclaim their Czech loyalty. Seven years is a long time, and many Czechs worked side by side with the Nazis. Now these collaborators, fearful of their countrymen seeking reprisals, took up arms and fought the exhausted backs of what remained of the German army. A German family that had lived in our village long before the war suddenly found itself swarmed by vengeful Czechs. Their German identity would have been enough to condemn them, but there were rumours propelled by idle tongues that the patriarch of this family had fed information to the local Nazi authority. Their house under siege, the German father and mother pled in vain with the angry crowd to let them leave with the retreating troops. Into the midst of this mob stepped Petr Ludek. He was in his late twenties, and he and his wife Zdeňa had a little girl and boy not much younger than me. He tried to calm the crowd, but his supplications to reason and Christian ideals were met with shouts for blood. Convinced that the crowd would not set the house aflame if he, an innocent Czech, was inside, Ludek proclaimed he would stay with the German family until the crowd had overcome its madness. Before he closed the door, he beckoned any other like-minded Czechs to join him inside. None did. The next morning, the house was in ashes and Petr Ludek and the German family were dead.

As I grew older this story became more distant and I thought of it less and less. It was only when Soviet troops marched into our country and I watched men climb onto tanks and cry out injustice that the memory of Petr Ludek returned to me. As is with many memories of childhood, it is the idea that prevails over the details. Points of history melt away into impression and myth. And so from this incident of the burnt German family emerged Petr Ludek. The naïve defender of goodness. I cannot remember what he looked like, but I have seen his incarnation hundreds of times. His manifested spirit roams about Prague and infects the young and old with the treacherous ideas of principle, virtue, and goodness.

He is, apart from his name, a figment of my imagination, while Zdeňa is his female counterpart. So I return to my question: why keep faithful to goodness? The answer I have reached, but would prefer not to accept, is this: Petr Ludek chooses to be good. He confronts injustice, he gives alms to the poor, and he places himself in danger to rescue cats out of trees. He fights for freedom using words and peaceful action. He is always kind to women and makes love to them tenderly. He lives without the extravagant comforts of our time and offers his bed to travellers just as he takes the floor. He is a man without selfishness or vanity. But why does Petr do these things? There are two answers, neither of which is adequate. One is stupidity; the other is hope. I suggest stupidity because only a dullard will not see the faults of this world and continues to rescue cats from trees or give alms to the poor. But that is all that stupidity would achieve. The recognition of injustice; to identify oppression and fight for freedom, these are not the products of stupidity, rather they are the culmination of hours of analysis, debate, and moral struggle. These are not the activities of a stupid man, and so this first answer is indeed inadequate. Does Petr Ludek have hope? Yes. He has hope in the Garden of Eden, in the fantasy of a future without sin, one where history no longer repeats itself. And in this way, Petr is the real Marxist. No one will starve, no one will oppress another, and all men will walk as brothers. And yet now he finds himself hunted by the Party who claims ownership of such ideals. That is because if all men walked as brothers then no man would hold power over the other and no state—communist, fascist or republic—will ever condone such a utopia. Petr so believes in this fantasy that it pours from him. It directs his actions and it refuses inaction. It torments him but brings him to his own salvation. His faith in goodness lies in his hope for the future.

This is why I despise Petr Ludek. I do not believe in his vision of the future. I have no such garden sowed within my mind. The end of history was written in its beginning and our choices will continue to keep paradise at bay. Here we all unwillingly live in the darkness of the garden of men.

If it is such dreams of paradise that hold people to goodness, such comfortable delusions that drive one to do good, then Petr, Zdeňa, and all the names are no better than me or the Party. They invoke goodness because it will lead them to a fulfilled fantasy and appease their insecurity. And yet they condemn me, just as the Soviets condemn them. Perhaps that is my point. What drives me to madness is the hypocrisy of Petr and Zdeňa. Come down from your delusional clouds and live in this garden of men, where we toil and struggle and understand that this is the way it has been and shall always be.

The Downside of Cynicism

As I had no refuge from the ghosts of people forgotten and I did not want to be reminded of my brutishness in the arms of Anežka, I went to the cinema. Whenever I go to the cinema I am rarely drawn into the film, preferring to watch the people around me and see how the simulated feelings on the screen are so expectantly appropriated by the crowd. The film was in Russian with Czech subtitles. It was a tale of a

Russian platoon, undermanned and outgunned, liberating a small Ukrainian village from the Nazis. The point of the film as I perceived it was that with revolutionary zeal and sacrifice to the common good, the most unlikely of goals can be attained. The climax of the film came when a beloved soldier was shot by an evil German. As he gasped his last breaths I could not help but turn around. The blue light of the screen fell upon the audience and made running shadows on their rapturous faces. One woman had tears rolling down her fat cheeks, her eyes unshakable from the screen. As I watched her, I was mesmerized by her ability to lose herself in the story, as if the dying soldier was her own son. This stupid woman, who cried for actors on a sound stage far away from any danger and who were paid by the State to pontificate to rebellious nations, repulsed me. I heard a laugh echo in the movie house and in the same moment realized that the crying fat lady was staring at me. I scanned the rest of the crowd, whose eyes were all fixed on me, and realized that the inexplicable laughter was my own. As the audience began to deride me, I tried to recall the last time I had laughed, but could not.

I left the cinema as quickly as I could. The crowd yelled and jeered at me; enraged that the climax of the film should be so disturbed. I had not meant to laugh so callously at the crying fat woman. I did not feel ashamed (if anyone should have felt shame it was she), but I was surprised at my spontaneous and unrecognizable laughter. It had not been a laugh of joy of humour, but that of a desperate man uncertain whether to cry or laugh. That morning I had been given a list of men and women who would be made to disappear for no reason except that they had been identified, and no one—not I, nor the fat woman, nor the attendant who gave me my ticket, nor

Jitka—really cared. And yet in the theatre sat a group of people whose empathy had become overwhelmed by the suffering of the dying soldier, the product of some Soviet propaganda bureaucrat. I was not reproaching the crying woman because she had cried, but because she did not do so for the list of names. (Though had she, I would have simply called her a hysteric and let her cry.) Perhaps she found reality indigestible and only manicured emotion could evoke her sensibilities. And then I wondered if my laughter had not been to mock her, but rather to laugh at the sorry state of myself. Had not the voice risen outside of myself, unrecognizable until the audience identified me? Certainly if I rebuked the woman for her hypocrisy, I ought to reproach myself a dozenfold. And the more I thought of it, the more convinced I became that it was the saints who had sent that cold laughter into the cinema.

As I walked down the streets of Prague under the buzzing glow of the streetlights, I passed a group of laughing students. The sound was light and it bounced off the walls and filled the street. Once I had passed them I stepped into an alley and watched them stagger down the street. Two of the friends were obviously drunk, with the others holding them upright. They slapped each other's backs as they imprudently joked about the Russians and mocked Moscow. A cloud of laughter followed them down the street and echoed long after they had passed.

It had been a palpable cheer that roared and hovered above where I stood, and yet I could not take hold of it. I thought of my pitiless laugh at the cinema. From what place and memory had it stemmed? What cause had the saints to accost me so? I thought of the crying fat woman and the emotions in her eyes, and I could not bear to think that this woman was privy to an existence that was lighter and better than my own.

I continued my walk long after the echo of the students' laughter had dissipated into the night air and the street lay once again quiet and empty. I walked along the darkened cobblestones, searching for the intangible evocation of emotion that had come so easily to the people at the cinema. I passed by a courtyard where inside I caught the glimpse of a young couple sitting on the edge of a dry fountain. I slunk into the courtyard's entranceway and watched them from the shadows. They did not see me; they only saw each other. I could not hear what they were saying but on this damp night here they sat, enraptured with one another. She inched closer to him and slid her head to rest on his shoulder. They were young, perhaps in their early twenties, and their laughter held the comforting innocence that can only come when two people are in love for the first time. As I watched them from the shadows, I noticed that the chiselled faces of cherubs and saints lined the doorway where I stood. Their stone eyes glared at me as though to chase me from the scene, afraid that I would infect these young lovers with my cynicism. These two people, whose laughter expressed an unconditional trust in each other and in the belief that life should be filled with happiness and laughter and so at this moment, they claimed that right. I turned, and with a last glance at the lovers, stepped from the shadows and back into the dark street.

I spent much of that night wandering and listening for laughter, unable to remember a time when I had felt such gladness that it poured from me. I walked alone through the darkness, followed by the tap of my shoes against the cobblestones. In an early hour I followed a wave of laughter to a group of Russian soldiers who were sharing a bottle of vodka. They appraised me, first with the guilty expression of children caught in mischief, then with irritation. I smiled and made as if to leave them to their fun, but from the dark I continued to watch. Their voices were boisterous, bouncing through the streets like a release after sombre days. The Russian laughter rose and mixed with same Prague air that had been filled with the sounds of the students and the lovers. Even they seemed to understand something that evaded me.

I thought of Petr Ludek. I thought of him laughing as he sat with his friends and they debated intellectual trivialities. Of him laughing with Zdeňa as they drank coffee in the late afternoon sun. I thought of Anežka, how I had hurt her. I thought of my sad victory over the fantasy of Petr and Zdeňa. At this moment, it was they who had won and I who had lost, and yet they could not even care to claim their victory. Here I wandered through the streets, searching for something that I had never known was missing, while all the Petr Ludeks and Zdeňa Havlovás were laughing in their sleep, oblivious to the torment of a lowly Party bureaucrat that held their memory in his hands.

As dawn broke over the city, I walked up Prokopskă Street and up the stairs to my flat. I had searched all night to find laughter. I had heard it; drunken laughter, the laughter of friendship, of love, of fraternity. I had heard it so close to me but just beyond my grasp. All night it had eluded me and as I washed my face I thought of the crying fat woman in the cinema, and with my entire being I wished to trade my soul for hers.

The Laughing Butcher and His German Wife

I AM NOT A PERSON THAT REQUIRES MUCH SLEEP, and so I was surprised to find my head heavy and my eyelids weighted as I sat at my desk, a pile of papers before me. But I knew it was not tiredness that exhausted me but sadness. The day before at the cinema it had been cold mockery that had emanated from me. It was not my own laugh, it was that of a villain. Indeed I had come to play the role of villain in the story of Petr Ludek. But it was not this thought that bothered me; history necessitates villains. It was that I had become the villain in the story of my own life. And it had begun to consume me.

Grey clouds had once again moved into the city and rain tapped against my office window as I stared at the pile of names, each one imprinted on my brain. Slowly I took an empty warrant and slid it into the typewriter. My fingers began typing, creating a harsh counterpoint to the gentle rhythm of raindrops hitting my windowpane. My fingers tapped and my eyes read the names: the dates of birth, addresses, names of spouses and children, occupations, and their offences.

Svatopluk, Pavel
d.o.b: June 23, 1939;
5494 Otylie Ave., Klašterarec;
Children:
Stanislav - d.o.b. August 3, 1964
Magdalena - d.o.b. December 10, 1967
Eliška - d.o.b. July 10, 1963
Spouse - Svatoplukova, Hannah (ne Holstova)
butcher
Counter-revolutionary activities.

Pavel stood before me, his German wife beside him holding their nine-month-old daughter, while Eliška and Stanislav stood by my desk, their big brown eyes looking up at me, barely tall enough to see over the stacks of papers there. Eliška stood with her fingers resting on the desk as though she was trying to propel herself upward so she could see me. They all had their eyes locked on me. My every breath, every move, recorded in the reflection of their eyes. None of them spoke a word, asked for understanding or supplicated for pity. They simply stood with accusing eyes and clenched lips.

"I've forgotten how to laugh," I said.

They stood quietly, without moving, without retracting their collective stare.

"I don't understand why you're on this list."

Still they stood before me, the only response coming from the rain against the windowpane. I sat as a child might sit before a principal or teacher after behaving badly. But I told myself that I had behaved properly, and that I had nothing to apologize for. And so I told them so.

Then the butcher and his wife began to laugh. Their laughter rose and filled the room, and it roared into my ears. It was a laugh that penetrated the walls and drifted into the street. I put my hands to my ears but the laughter grew louder. The butcher and his German wife stood before me, their lives in my hands, and they laughed at me. Rage flowed from my toes to my head and back again. I felt their laughter rise up beyond the grey clouds and into a place that I did not know, and yet they remained in the room with me; the butcher and his German wife, on their knees, laughing.

I took the sheet from my typewriter and placed it with the few other warrants that I had completed that morning, then I rose and walked toward Jitka's desk, passing the butcher and his German wife, whose children now broke into raucous laughs that threatened to shatter the windows. I slapped the papers in front of Jitka with a gleeful vengeance and, before she could respond, turned and went back to my office. The room was empty and quiet. I closed the door behind me and turned to the window. The rain was falling heavily, washing the city clean. The droplets fell over the anonymous buildings, and I thought of the butcher, his German wife and their children. The world seemed empty. There was no laughter in my office, no sadness, only something that once resembled a man. I turned from the window and sat down at my desk. I looked over the list of names and, pulling an empty warrant through the typewriter, began typing once again.

Untitled Hero

When I left the office, it was still raining. I had not brought an umbrella and I walked under the heavy clouds for most of the way, only jumping on the streetcar once. I was tired and the rain woke me. The world seemed less angry with me now as people dashed back and forth and hid their faces under the domes of umbrellas. Prague had returned to normal, though an unintelligible anxiety hung over everything and seemed to keep sunlight at bay.

As I stepped into my apartment building I was accosted by a hysterical Lida Vrbecová, though she was rarely anything but. She was an older woman with grey and white hair, a very round bust, and rather short legs. Her children had grown and left her to the misery of a solitary life.

"Oh Mr. Svērák, oh Mr. Svērák," she panted as she ran toward me, her breasts bouncing up and down like two gelatinous hams. She began to regale me with the story of Lady Zuza, her cat, who was now stuck in the garbage chute. She blathered on, telling me all the ailments that plagued her old age. If only she were young and healthy like me, she would have promptly crawled into the garbage chute and rescued the poor kitten herself. Then, like many Slavic women of her age who possess the unique ability to represent their lives as being simultaneously much worse and much better than your own, she told me of how the rain tormented her arthritis. This still did not have the desired effect of eliciting an offer from me to go into the garbage chute and rescue Lady Zuza, and so she stuttered and stumbled, searching for new tales to entice my good heartedness. Unfortunately for her, Mrs. Vrbecová did not know anything about my nature. I had no deep aversion to going into the garbage chute after the cat, but my silence came from a desire to make her ask. But Mrs. Vrbecová was stubborn and did not want to have to make an official request. "Mr. Svērák, you don't understand my troubles." She proceeded to tell me about her son, who it seems was unable to find a "good woman." Mrs. Vrbecová was so concerned for her son that she had bought him a new suit so he could impress the young ladies, but it was out of style. Outraged by his mother's faux pas, her son had thrown the suit at her and refused to ever visit again. "I am an old woman, what do I know of what is fashionable these days? I try, I try and he throws it in my face, as if it meant nothing. Nothing. And now I will never see him again and Lady Zuza is in the garbage chute." Her hand stroked her head as if to emphasize this last point, as though the weight of her troubles had left her light headed and on death's doorstep. The tale of the suit was ridiculous and so to avoid another one I quickly offered to rescue Lady Zuza.

The chute was an old dumbwaiter that Mrs. Vrbecová had made clear was not to be used, though I knew that the irritatingly noisy couple on the fourth floor used it all the time. I unenthusiastically grasped the rope and pulled the dumbwaiter up to the chute entrance where I stood. Muttering to myself a number of obscenities regarding Mrs. Vrbecová's impotent son, I crawled through the small door and into the shaft. It was tight in the chute, and I was cold from my wet clothes, still dripping with rainwater. I lowered myself on the dumbwaiter. The pulleys squeaked loudly and I wondered how it was that they carried my weight. It was dark and the only light that shone into the long shaft came from the cracks between the small doors that sat on each floor. The putrid stench of rotting sardines assailed my nose and I hurried in pulling myself to the upper floors. I kept an open ear for the cry of a cat and occasionally called out her name, but I did not see nor hear any sign of Lady Zuza. Once I reached the top of the shaft, the bulky bottom of the dumbwaiter blocked any line of light from illuminating the chute and I sat in complete darkness. I found it tenuously comforting, as though I could easily slip into the numbing void. In the absolute darkness of the garbage chute I was invisible to all, even to myself.

"Mr. Svērák, what's taking you so long?" Mrs. Vrbecová's loud voice echoed through the chute, which magnified the irritating intonations of her voice. I sighed in the darkness and with the pulleys squeaking resumed my search for Lady Zuza. I had pulled myself up and down twice over the whole height of the chute before I heard her muffled call. I found her perched in a small alcove from where the intense stench of rotten sardines emanated. She seemed relieved to see me, jumping from the alcove and into my arms without hesitation. She was a black cat, though her face and paws were marked by large white spots, as if she had walked through a tub of white paint. I wrapped my arm around her and with my free hand pulled myself to the nearest exit.

Lady Zuza clung to me as I handed her to the now-ecstatic Mrs. Vrbecová who had to pry the cat off my arm with some difficulty. She showered me with thanks, but was sure to tell me that once when her son had gone hunting for Lady Zuza in the garbage chute he had returned with her in half the time it had taken me. As I walked up the stairs to my apartment I thought of Mrs. Vrbecová's son and his troubles with women, of Mrs. Vrbecová and Lady Zuza. With chattering teeth and the smell of rotten sardines hanging about me, I let a smile creep onto my face.

On the Inconvenience of Blindness

I slept well into the night, my brain taking refuge in the amusement that Mrs. Vrbecová and Lady Zuza had afforded me. When I awoke it was close to dawn. I stepped out of bed and went to open the window. It had stopped raining and the air smelled of a satisfied earth that was no longer thirsty. A breeze picked up and I felt its cool lick over my face as it entered the flat, eradicating the stale smell of a room left to sit for far too long. I let my arms rise to embrace the dawn and once again I smiled. As the first streaks of sun spread over the sky I resolved not to think about laughter or about Petr Ludek or about the butcher and his German wife. These were fixations whose questions I could not answer and whose queries pointed me to madness. I swore to the dawn that no longer would I search for these answers, and as the sun breached the sky, the smile that had crossed my face disappeared.

Typing the complete list took the remainder of the week, and I was surprised how easily I completed the remaining warrants. As I typed and filed away name after name, I cannot say if their spirits were invoked as the butcher and his German wife had been, because I did not look up. I kept my eyes down to the paper and my ears open only to the bell of the typewriter that chimed as each line was completed. It's quite remarkable what a man can accomplish if he keeps his head and eyes down.

When I finished the list, I gave the filled warrants to Jitka, who took them with her usual lack of warmth. It was a Friday and so I decided to call Anežka to see if she would have dinner with me that night. To my great pleasure she accepted, and we dined at the lounge. I did not feel that she required an explanation for our last encounter, and as expected she made no reference to it. We ate dinner and spoke of the rain and other trivialities, but for the greater part of the evening we sat in silence. It was not unusual nor did I find it uncomfortable. Occasionally as she looked down at her plate, I let my eyes linger on her. She wore a red dress that cradled her bosom and draped over her petite figure with a sophisticated elegance. As we approached her room for the evening's culmination I felt extraordinarily at ease, and I would have laughed, but laughter still evaded me. As we entered her room and Anežka undressed, it turned into a strange discomfort, as though I were invoking the memory of something that best lay buried. I put it out of my mind, lay down on the bed beside her and began to softly caress her neck and breasts. The smell of her hair and the taste of her skin carried the memory of the many times I had held her, but there was something else. I knew what it was but dared not acknowledge it, so I continued kissing her body. But beneath the surface I could feel the determined indifference of her mind. She had trained her body to do what her mind was unwilling to, and here I was, like some beast in the wilderness, claiming ownership over something that was not mine in the least.

Still I persisted, my hands roaming over her in a primal grope of lust. But the more lustful my hands became the less my mind was willing and I realized that I was as limp as a dumpling. I renewed my attempt, but the more I tried with Anežka, the more frustrated I became. I had never had such a problem and felt ashamed that I should expose my manhood so carelessly. Again I tried, but all I could think of was Anežka's mind, somewhere hidden in the body under me, waiting to come out when all was done. As I thought of it, I became convinced that Petr Ludek and Zdeňa were in the room with me and a sharp mocking laughter grew in my ears. I sat up and saw Petr and Zdeňa, standing hand in hand in the centre of the room, laughing at me. "I thought I put you away," I whispered. They did not answer; they only laughed. It was the same sound that had come from the butcher and his German wife, the same pitiful disdain at my attempts to be a man.

Anežka brought me back. She asked what was wrong in a sweet voice, and though I did not know if she was sincere, she was not laughing. I pondered the question for a moment, but having not been asked such a question in some time I did not know how to answer, and at this the laughter grew. A hundred people now stood the room, laughing, some rolling on the floor in hysterics, some quietly chuckling in contentment, some bellowing and heaving. I could name each one. I knew their dates of birth, their children's names, their occupations, their illegal activities. For each name that had been etched into my brain through that horrible list was a face that mocked me, faces that could triumph because righteousness was theirs and not mine. I looked down at Anežka. Her eyes were full of tenderness, and a curiosity into my condition that comforted me. And because I had forgotten how to laugh, how to make love, how to answer a simple question, I fell into Anežka's arms and cried. And the crowd disappeared.

I MET ANEŽKA ALMOST TWO YEARS AGO. I had just been through a string of very brief affairs, and was exhausted by the outpouring of attention that these women demanded. Plans constantly had to be formulated, days and even weeks in advance, and after a while I could not be bothered to feign interest anymore and soon reclaimed the happy solitude of my flat. I went with a friend (at the time I still had a small group of friends, but they dispersed and grew families and now do not have time to go drinking) to the lounge where Anežka spent so much of her time. My friend and I sat at a table and drank copiously. We were joined by Anežka and her colleague and soon we were all smoking and laughing. I had not looked at Anežka with much admiration, but neither did I condescend to her for what she did to make her living. Since then, our relationship, while amicable, has been about little more than the satiation of lust. I often took her out to eat, or we would go for a stroll. Once we even went dancing. But we never spoke of the true nature of our relationship, and despite its illegality it was well understood between the two of us that I was client and paying for her presence. Sometimes I would think of it, but it was the way of things, and I could not, nor did I want, to change them. I never asked why she had become a prostitute, nor did she ever feel the need to explain herself to me. And so we continued.

I left Anežka's room shortly after I had shed my tears. I thanked her and apologized, but she explained I needn't and that sometimes men wanted her to hold them like a mother rather than a lover. I did not find this particularly comforting, but thanked her again and, leaving some crowns on the nightstand, walked as quickly as I could out into the street. Here I felt as though once again I could breathe, that the world was opening up for me again; away from laughter, away from Anežka, away from the dizzying accusations of Petr Ludek and the others. I walked briskly through the dark streets, replaying the evening's events in my mind.

A wave of laughter crashed out of a bar and into the street and I thought that I would be sick if I heard any more, so I broke into a sprint. I arrived to the dark silence of my apartment and rested. My covenant with the dawn had been broken, and now I could think of nothing else but Petr Ludek, and the list of names, and how Anežka had held me while I cried like a child at her bosom. Shame and embarrassment overcame me and I felt ill. I walked to the window and opened it to let the cool fall air chase away the demons.

The city was quiet below me. Five stories down, a small square speck in the courtyard denoted the bust of Lenin. I thought of how, not so long ago, the bust had been Stalin, and then before that Masaryk, and before that Saint Zdislava. How quickly the city changes. Are Prague's walls and sidewalks so malleable, so impressionable? And yet I had spoken with Mrs. Vrbecová shortly after workers had changed Stalin to Lenin, and she did not even remember that the bust had ever been anything but Lenin. Does one forget an inconvenient history? Erase it because to remember would bear inconvenient consequences for the present? Eradicate the past to accept the future and hope that the saints will forgive omission and grant us a sinless future? So it seemed with Mrs. Vrbecová, and I could not deny that it was also the case with me.

I closed the window, the cool breeze no longer a comfort, and pulled out a bottle of brandy. I drank and smoked until sleep overcame me and I stumbled to my bed, my clothes still on my body and the smell of Anežka lingering in my nose and on my fingertips. I fell into a melancholy sleep, full of half-dreams and demonic visitations. In my drunkenness I dreamt of a bust, perched high up on a pedestal. I could not see whose image rested on top and so I jumped up and down trying with all my might to learn who it was. The butcher and his German wife appeared and effortlessly floated up to see it, but still I could not. In my aggravation I began to rock the pedestal back and forth until the bust tumbled down and broke into hundreds of pieces. I scavenged the remains to see who it had been, but all that remained was dust. I turned to the pedestal, which now rose as a pillar to the sky, and wrapping my arms and legs around it, began to climb. Higher and higher I went, until the ground disappeared and I could see the entire city of Prague. Where men looked like ants and walls looked like sand forged by changing winds. Finally reaching the top, I stood up where once the unknown bust had been. I began to laugh, a big, bellowing laugh that filled the air and the city. Then, with the surprise of an unfortunate visitor, Jitka appeared. My laughter ceased and I fell on my knees begging for her forgiveness. She snickered and then without a word pushed me off the pedestal. I awoke with a paralyzing fear and for an hour I trembled in bed before gaining the courage to rise.

The Malleable Face of Petr Ludek

My weekends usually pass with little of note, and this weekend began as no exception. Once I had attributed my dream to silliness, I ventured out into the budding day for breakfast and coffee. Afterward, a clear blue sky and glaring sun drew out compact shadows and I made my way to my mother's as I often did on Saturdays. She lived in a small flat at the bottom of an odious new Soviet-funded highrise that sat on Odbojný Avenue. The day was growing warmer, and the sunshine cascaded onto the city and made that which would otherwise be ordinary beautiful. I decided to take the long way to my mother's flat and walk along the river. The sunbeams beat down onto my skin, rejuvenating me and driving away the hangover and the fearful echo of my dream.

The Vltavá River runs almost five hundred kilometres from its southern source, bending north through Prague till it feeds into the Elbe and onto Dresden and Hamburg, finally completing its journey at the North Sea. Life breaks forth, carves through the landscape of established history, collects tributaries of memory—happiness, resentment, regret—and then slips into the great abyss of the sea. And yet here the river passed before me, reflecting the sunlight onto stone overpasses in fractured prisms, marching forward in a steady momentum. I stood at its edge, my eyes following a swirl of water across the panorama, until the heat of the sun forced me to find shelter under the shade of a tree. Finding a bench, I slid out of my coat and rolled up my sleeves. With the Charles Bridge providing a picturesque backdrop, I sat and watched the people. Some went about their errands, barely noticing the sun and the river and the chirping birds. Others strolled about, stopping to admire the view and bask in the warmth. A woman pushing a pram stopped to check on her crying child. A young man held the hand of a blonde woman who looked to be quite older than he. An old man strolled, hands in his pockets, his face pensive. Time passed, and the sun moved across the sky, and still I sat on the bench with the clear blue sky beaming its bright reflection into the Vltavá. A woman came by selling bread and I bought some, eating it and sharing it with the pigeons who multiplied at my feet, their soft coos soothing my mind. I thought of all that had transpired over the past week and it seemed more than had happened all year. With the sun on my face I tried to let the images of prams, old men, and young lovers wash away any disagreeable thoughts, but I could not help but wonder if any of these people were on the list of names. Perhaps the woman with the carriage was Ludmilla Drahoslavová, or the blonde woman with the much younger man was the butcher's German wife visiting her lover in the city. Perhaps the young student was one of the many incarnations of Petr Ludek. They moved perilously forward, not knowing that their futures had already been written, warrants had already been issued. Part of me sat in a curious fascination that they should be so oblivious, and yet another part implored me to run up to them, take them by the hand and lead a mass exodus from Czechoslovakia. But I remained seated on the bench, watching and waiting for someone to accuse me of wrong. But none did.

In the late afternoon I decided to make my way to Maminka's, my caution and apprehension growing as I knew she had been expecting me hours earlier. I hurried across the bridge and jumped on a bus that took me to the new concrete apartment complexes that lay on the far side of the city, and which stood as testaments to Communism's dreary practicality. In fact it had been I who had gotten this flat for my mother when she moved to Prague. As I was a member of the Housing Relocation Committee, it had been simple for me to assign her a place that was not too far from, but not too close to my own home. When I arrived at long last, Maminka was angrier than I had anticipated. Even as I knocked, I heard her muffled voice on the other side call out: "This best not be my stupid son." I said nothing and soon heard her pull the latch of the door.

"Maminko," I said when the door was open, half in greeting, half in supplication. She waddled back to her small living room and resumed her position in front of the television. I closed the door behind me and made my way after her. I had bought a small bouquet of flowers as a peace offering, but she simply slapped them down beside her on the small sofa, keeping her eyes locked on the television screen and her arms crossed over her bosom. I rolled my eyes and looked into the kitchen. Food sat along the small kitchen counter, her fine blue china was set out in a stately row. She had risen early, gone to the market, hurried home and prepared my favourite meal, only to wait for hours. My heart ached at the hope and anticipation she had poured into every dumpling and every crushed garlic clove. In the face of her excitement, my lax tardiness made her efforts seem foolish to her. A blue china plate piled with dumplings, now cold, sat on the counter. She had garnished the plate with parsley and this too she thought I would take note of and commend her for the bourgeois appearance she had given the meal. At this we would laugh, and then we would eat the food she had prepared and share a bottle of beer, and for a time, she could reclaim the past. Those dumplings with parsley garnish made my entire being mourn for my mother's failed afternoon dinner.

I knelt down before her and took her hand in mine. I told her that I was sorry and that lately I had much on my mind and so had spent the day walking and thinking. She looked at me and her stern grimace melted. She patted my cheek and said she forgave me. Her eyes were so full of tenderness that I had to look away for fear that tears would form in my own.

Maminka leaned over the countertop, warming the dumplings, pork roast, and sauerkraut. I watched her as she puttered between the counter and table, where she had insisted I sit and rest. She had become remarkably frail over the past few years. Not in weight or agility, but in her shuffle and stature, the way she held her head and forged her smile. Her endlessly blue eyes still twinkled, though with a sobriety that had not been there before, as if her gaze were lost in a place no one else could see. As I watched her, her present frailty clashed with the memory of her determined stride. The way that she had marched into my school, demanding to know why my teacher had beaten me. Or the steadiness of her hands and voice when she told me my father had died. Or the laughter that rang from her as she chased me through the buttercup layered meadows of our old home. The memories stood apart from the white hair and wrinkled skin that now seemed almost translucent, as though she were disappearing.

At last Maminka sat down at the table and I gratefully ended my drift into memory. She placed a steaming plate of *vepřo-knedlo-zelo* before me as I poured the cold beer in our glasses (for every Czech knows that there is no superior combination than sauerkraut, dumplings, pork roast, and beer). "You know this would all taste much better if it had been eaten fresh. Now the roast is too dry," she said once we had begun eating.

I assured her the roast was not dry.

"And the dumplings, they too seem dry, or perhaps not soft enough."

I told her the dumplings were moist and fluffy, as she well knew they were. But it seems that in old age one searches for praise much like one did as a child. It amused me to think of the reversal of roles, of how I now sat as a parent might before a child, humouring her leading questions and commentary.

"So what do you spend your days doing that makes you forget your mother for hours? I've always said you think too much," she said, holding the fork as though she were underlining her assertion.

But now I did not know what to say. I could not tell her about the warrants, or Anežka, or anything that pressed upon my mind, and so "work," was all I said, and she knew not to question me further. She was aware that I no longer worked for the Housing Ministry and had been moved to the ironically named Justice Ministry. She had been informed of this by the nosy Mrs. Blažková, who kept abreast of all the goings-on of everyone who had come from our small village. We momentarily sat in a silence that spoke of the questions she wanted to ask, but whose answers she did not want to hear. So instead she talked about the neighbours and their imbecile son and the dirty sidewalks in this part of Prague.

After dinner we sat on the sofa in front of her small television sipping my uncle's medovina. As we sipped, the liqueur loosened her tongue and Maminka spoke of our old home, something she rarely did unless induced by drink. I sat beside her, wishing her to be silent lest she let loose the unbearable heaviness that comes when nostalgia is evoked. Nostalgia: it is a worm that burrows into your brain and recalls stale joys made untouchable by time. But she did set it loose, and she spoke in intermittent sighs of the smell of the woodstove as it was stoked by my father on a deep winter night. She spoke of me, and the silly things I did when I could barely walk or speak. She spoke of the signs of life that spring brought each year; the dandelions, buttercups, and phlox that flooded the hills and meadows she roamed in childhood, as brooks swelled and rushed down into the valleys in moving ribbons of white water. Her eyes were focused on the dark television screen whose only image was the pale reflection of her and me sitting on a musty couch with sherry glasses in our hands. It was a sad image, made sadder still because Maminka had all but disappeared, lost to the abyss of perfect memory. With each word I felt my heart grow heavier, my legs restless and my hands anxious. Beauty is trampled on in age, and to be reminded of such atrocity can hardly be borne. As my mother fell further and further into this perfect past that may or may not have ever existed, she turned to me and her eyes were wet with tears. I looked at her and all I could see was the echo of a joy long dissipated. She alone was sustained by this memory of a time forgotten by all except her. "You remember. Remember how happy we were?" she asked.

I thought and I remembered. Something perhaps. If it was happiness, I did not want to know and did not want to remember. But I looked into her eyes and saw the desperation that age must breed. That yearning to know that a life has been happy. Hopes fulfilled. Dreams lived. Life has been worth living. And so I looked at her wrinkled face, her lips quivering, uncertain whether to smile or scream, and I gave her the contemptuous confirmation she desired—that happy memories were all that filtered into my brain, that the lamentable present was made bearable by the perfect past. She released a sigh of relief and fell back into her chair. Her muscles relaxed and her mind drifted into the hourglass. My head fell and my eyes dipped into the golden colour of the mead in my glass. I could not help but feel that I was partially to blame, that in some way I had caused her brevity of joy. And so I lifted my glass and swallowed the sorrow of a perfect past with the sweet liqueur.

Soon afterward, my restless legs were granted their wish and I found myself at the door sliding into my coat. Maminka had risen from her chair and now stood beside me. "Time moves too quickly," she said. A statement on life rather than our afternoon, I supposed. She reached for me, her soft hands holding my arms, and looked into my face. Her endless blue eyes, glazed with the living memory of the past, searched mine, for what I did not know. But with each passing moment I felt a greater discomfort. And as she looked, it was my discomfort that told her what she needed to know, and her hands rose to my face. Softened with age and yet calloused from a life of work, her hands pressed against my cheeks and gently held me. I dared not breathe for fear that words would escape my lips and I would speak of all that pressed so heavily on my mind. To speak of the things that plagued me, to speak of that which condemned me, to pour them out like water as though I were a child again. But with the greatest effort I kept silent. She wrapped her arms around me and held me tightly, as she had done time and time again, and said no more.

As I walked into the dark street, I felt a heavy sorrow, an implacable feeling that stemmed from the knowledge that happiness was impossible for Maminka. Her faith was in the past. There lay her garden. It had grown and then died too quickly. And though it caused her torment, it was also that which made her present tolerable. I momentarily paused in the middle of the street, my eyes gazing down on dirty sidewalk slabs, and wondered why my faith was so depleted, why neither the past, nor the present, nor the future provided me with solace. As I thought of these questions I felt that I was being followed. The street was empty behind me, but I knew that in the shadows and the darkness lurked the ghosts of names that would be forgotten by all but me.

—

I RESUMED MY WALK through the darkened and foggy streets. I did not want to think about being followed, about the names, or about Maminka. I wanted to think of the breeze on my face, the smell of the air; oh the bliss of the soul untainted by the world. I did not want to take the streetcar or the bus because I could not sit still. I did not look up or around me, but kept my eyes on the passing crevices between the slabs of sidewalk. The sound of my shoes echoed in the fog that had rolled in from the river and momentarily banished the void of silence that encased the city. It was a Saturday night but so quiet that each singular sound that snuck through the fog declared its solitude in a diffusing echo.

I stumbled through the fog until before me emerged a series of stone steps that rose toward the carved wooden doors of a church. As I approached, a window of clear air opened and the church doors materialized into an ornate wall of emboldened saints and prophets. Each held their eyes to the heavens, each declared themselves holy. I stood before the magnificent structure for some time. But it seemed that the saints paid no attention to me. I looked about, and in an imprudent moment mounted the steps that led to the church door.

I expected the door to be locked but, at the urging of my arm, it fell open and I slid inside. Only at such a time of night, in this darkness, would I have dared enter a church. For a Party official to do so is very dangerous, and an indictable offence. To my relief the church was empty. Candles cast flickering shadows that danced in the draft of my entrance. Above me rose an immense dome that seemed to reach out of the darkness and merge with the open sky.

As I moved through the vacant structure, each footfall became a proclamation of solitude. I stood still and let the darkness welcome me. The image of a living saint stood before me, moving in the candlelight to mimic an unsteady dance of life. I did not know which saint it was, but his impressive form took me by surprise. Enraptured eyes looked upward to the heavens, as if he were witness to something which eluded the rest of us. Lines of lit candles at his feet cast a flickering glow on his face, and the light bent shadows to feign changing expressions. Over his heart was etched a single flame, painted in a chipping gold that revealed the saint's wooden interior. It too bounced and danced in the reflected light of the candles. I stood beneath him, watching this disciple of the divine. I waved my hand over the candles and watched the expressions change on his face. Sorrow. Anger. Joy. Excitement. The candlelight played on his face until the air and the flames stood still. I looked at him as he looked upward with no thought but to God. Through his fluctuating expressions, his eyes remained locked to the church ceiling. There lay his hope. There lay his faith.

The stillness of the church was broken by the grumble of a door. Footsteps echoed in the empty dome and fear took my gut and nailed my feet to the ground. As the intruder came closer, I slunk behind a stone pillar that rose to the arching dome. My body broke into a cold sweat and I wondered what had possessed me to ever come into this condemned place.

A voice echoed in the darkness. "You don't have to hide. I know you're there."

I said nothing.

"I'm the rector here." He paused. "Not a policeman."

It seemed I had little choice but to take the voice at its word. He was alone, and that afforded me the security to venture out from the shadows and into the dim candlelight. I looked at the man. He was older than me, with grey encroaching on what sporadic brown hair remained on his head. He had a round face, with circular glasses that jutted out and rested on the tip of his nose. On his neck he wore the collar of a priest. I apologized for my intrusion and moved toward the door.

"You need not be afraid."

I told him I was not afraid.

He smiled and moved to sit down in a pew. "Everyone is afraid. The city is afraid. Anxiety grips the nation and the world trembles." He released a sigh with this last word as if he felt the fear and yet found it amusing.

I said nothing, and only thought of leaving.

"Were you afraid I was a policeman, or a priest?"

I said nothing for some time and thought the question curious. But then I did speak. "Is there a difference?"

He laughed, though he looked surprised. "Yes, in this world there is a difference."

"You are a policeman of God. You condemn, just as the Party condemns. You both choose your salvations. You both decide what is right and wrong."

The priest looked at me, eyebrows lifted in surprise. He rose to his feet, but it was not out of irritation or anger. I stepped back as he approached.

"God does not condemn. It is we who condemn ourselves."

"Believe in the Party and they will not condemn."

"But does the Party give us salvation, eternal salvation?"

"It claims to. Just as you claim it."

"And what of truth?"

I paused for a moment, reluctant to continue, but I did. "There is no such thing."

"And goodness?"

"I don't know what goodness means."

"What do you think it means?" he asked.

Reluctantly, I told him what I thought. That it was a necessary creation of our nature to believe that goodness and perfection lay in our future, and lay in our past. That goodness was a fantasy taught to our children to make the present tolerable. That few benefits had ever come from proclamations of goodness, or selfless acts that, in the end, fell into the folds of humanity's historical continuum. "At the end of our civilization, there will be two oars for posterity: hope and sin. And because hope is predicated on the overcoming of sin, hope is, and was from its conception, a paradoxical entity. So what shall remain at the end of our time? Only sin. Only vice."

I finished my diatribe and the priest frowned. "Indeed if you have no faith…" He seemed lost in thought and, as we stood in the dark church, the giant dome hovering over us, I could not help but feel an affinity for this man who took my words with such sincerity. Part of me wished I had not spoken so harshly of his vision, for at that moment I was uncertain if I believed it myself. After a moment he continued. "What good have you done?"

I stood unsure how to respond, unsure if I should declare myself a Party bureaucrat and confess my part in condemning the names. But it was not a confession that he wanted, only to know what good I had done in this world, and it struck me that I could not think of anything. And so I said nothing.

The priest remained silent and we stood in the empty echo of flickering candles. Eventually he sat back in the pew. "Why be a virtuous man? This is the question of our existence. Philosophers, theologians, prophets have given us answers, but in the end none truly satisfies. Through all the words and fanciful ideals, there is only one thing that remains. Choice. To act. To speak out. To see. To hear. Choices are ours to make, for better or worse. Whether one acts or one sits back and lets the status quo continue; a choice has been made. It is you then who chooses to be good or not, you choose what is good or not." He rose then, and walked up to me, placing his hand on my shoulder. "This is God's gift to you." Slowly he turned and hobbled back into the darkness. He seemed slower and older than before, as if our conversation had aged him. I remained standing under the dome until anxiety lifted my legs and against my will propelled me into a sprint and carried me from the church.

—

When my feet had slowed, I found myself walking along the edge of the river once again, though now the world was dark and I could not see beyond the artificial glare of the streetlamps. Between my footfalls, I could hear the clock in the distance chime two and I wondered that I should have roamed so aimlessly through this hateful city. I thought of Maminka and I thought of the priest. Of Anežka and Petr Ludek and Zdeňa. Of the butcher and his German wife and Jitka. These characters danced through my mind, unabated by my physical tiredness, pushing me to madness. My conversation with the priest had been full of rational sincerity. The past forged our present, but did it also claim our will? I could not surrender to such an idea and found it curious that I should be so determined to prove that choice was mine and mine alone, given that such a conclusion would unequivocally condemn me.

Through my thoughts I caught sight of a man on a bench, his face buried in his hands, weeping. It was the same bench on which I had sat earlier that day, and as I approached I could hear his chokes and heaves, tears flowing over his cheeks. I froze on the walkway, watching him as he bawled to the river. For some time I stood there, considering him, and thinking of the words of the priest. What was it that had compelled this man to come here in the middle of the night to converse with the river in broken heaves? What had been the choices of his past that drove him to such hysterics? Yet I was here watching him. I had just cause to weep to the river, and yet I remained indifferent to those names that I had condemned. I wondered whether perhaps this was the reason for his weeping. That he knew the State would find him, and take his life. This was not Petr Ludek, and yet it was.

He spotted me, and jumped to his feet with an incredible energy. I had disrupted his confession. He was not Petr Ludek. He was me. A nameless bureaucrat who felt too much. Who did the Party's bidding out of fear, and yet felt each condemnation, each revoked freedom. He was a better man than I. For I did not weep, nor did I wish to weep. He stood away from me and his face flickered from sorrow, to anger, to fear like the saint in the church. I felt a great solidarity with this man. There was no sound between us but for his heavy breathing. Then, just a moment after having risen, he turned around and ran into the darkness, away from me, and away from the eyes that accused him of having a conscience.

Shortly afterward I followed his lead and made my way up Prokopskă Street, past the bust of Lenin, into my apartment building. My head and feet were tired and I fell into my bed, exhausted by thought. In my last waking moments, I thought of the sun on my face and the hands of Maminka, and the sincerity of the priest, and I knew that these things, these people, deserved my tears.

Petr Ludek Comes to Life

On Sunday I awoke, as I always did on Sundays, to the sound of church bells. The sun was shining through the open window and the opaque white curtain moved in a velvet breeze. The wind brushed over my face as I lay in bed, and the feeling that came over me was the same as you feel on returning home and watching the sun set over the familiar landscape of your homeland. Everything is bathed in an orange light and summons a stillness that holds your breath and whispers of a celestial world. Yet for all its beauty and for all the joy it brings forth, part of you is saddened because you remember the first time you gazed at the colours changing in the orange glow of the slumbering sun. And now as you watch it disappear beneath the rolling hills and pastures you remember that awe, and know it can never again be evoked. And so you are sad. That is the feeling that came over me in bed that morning, with the sound of bells in the clear blue Prague sky as the soft morning breeze blew through my bedroom window and onto my face.

I had breakfast in a café in Wenceslas Square where I read the morning's propaganda pieces. In front of me sat a couple; the man was my age, the woman the same, perhaps a little younger. As they looked over the menu they would turn and stare into each others' eyes, and then burst into idiotic laughter like adolescent children. They did this many times, and when the waiter came to take their order, they laughed even more. I could not understand why they were laughing, what it was they found so comical in their own faces. I sat and listened to their conversations on the silliest of topics: her mother, her dress, his mother, her friend Petra, who was as slim and flat-chested as a bean pole and sleeping with a Russian soldier. And yet as they both ate their breakfast and talked over these banal topics, there was something of substance here, an unspoken understanding of comfort and vulnerability. These stories were not meant for me, they were only meant for them. They were stories of love, not in and of themselves (if they were, then they were very stupid indeed), but rather the stories were tangible enactments of their love. This woman would not regale me with such accounts, nor would the man, for they were part of the private and unbreakable sphere that forms when a woman and a man love one another. And as I watched and listened I felt a sudden embarrassment for them, as though they were making love on the table in the bistro. I blushed at the thought, and quickly paid the bill. Before I left I looked at them once again, and instead of embarrassment, I felt a kind of sad happiness. And then I remembered the stale beauty and musty gladness evoked by the bells and the curtain floating on the breeze, and the same feeling ran through me. And in the midst of it I thought of Anežka.

I did not mean to go to the lounge, but I wandered in that direction all the same. Like the day before, the sun was shining brightly and people were out everywhere enjoying the last warm days of the year. I walked all over the city and as morning gave way to afternoon the temperature rose. I found myself carrying my coat and rolling my shirtsleeves, but even then I continued to sweat. I took up residence on a bench, and under the beating sun it was not long until I had fallen asleep. In my sleep, I dreamt of Anežka. As I had walked away from the couple in the bistro, my heart jumped at women who barely resembled her. And when groups of people passed, I could not help but scan their faces for her likeness. I censured myself for such foolish acts, but could not hold myself back from entertaining the hope that I might spend this day with her.

When I awoke from my nap the sun was already drawing out long shadows. My head felt light and dizzy from the heat and sun, but mostly from Anežka. She had invaded my dreams and now my waking life. Grabbing my jacket I set off with a brisk pace in the direction of the lounge. When I arrived I was once again sweating copiously and I waited for a moment before entering, adjusting my shirt and jacket, and running my fingers through my hair. I stepped in and the host brought me to my usual table. I had a drink, and waited for Anežka. Another girl, who I had not seen before, came and sat down next to me. I told her I was looking for Anežka and asked if she had come to the lounge that evening. Surprised, the girl said Anežka was in, and then rose to leave me to my preferred solitude. Time went on and Anežka did not appear. I knew that there were a few others who Anežka entertained at the lounge, but it was not so common that they would occupy so much of her time, and so early. She had once told me, in her smooth voice, that there were few other men who took so much of her time or treated her as well. I had forgotten that episode until I sat here now and it pleased me. The amount of pleasure I received from this memory was entirely disproportionate to what it had initially meant. But now as I sat here growing more impatient by the minute, the urge to see her grew exponentially and this memory afforded me a temporary indulgence. I did not want to take her to bed, but simply to see her, to speak with her. As the hours went by and I watched the men about me pawing the women, a growing feeling of isolation grew in me and I wondered how it was that I found myself in such a place as this. For I did not feel that I was like these men, and yet my presence proved the contrary.

It had been some time since I had felt the need for any kind of sentimental companionship. I had of course continued to seek physical partnership with Anežka, but had not required anything more from her, or anyone else. I had condemned sentimentality and love long before the Russians had invaded, found them tedious things and inconsequential to the life of a content bachelor. But now part of me yearned for something more, as if a feeling that had lain dormant for years had been woken by recent events. And despite my efforts to avoid the remembrance, I thought of Sabina. She had been the only woman I had ever thought of marrying; perhaps the only woman that I had ever loved. I think I did love her. In any case she was one of the few women with which I had held some semblance of a conventional relationship. Sabina had often spoken of her desire to have children and raise a family and initially I indulged her, suggesting that such was my own desire. I did this more from a sense of obligation, that this should have also been what I wanted, rather than from a desire to placate her. But after months of growing disinterest, Sabina left me, with a note in my flat charging me with immaturity and deception, her last word on our failed relationship. I had been negligent in my affection towards her. I knew this and admitted it freely (perhaps too freely). But I could not deny that I had breathed a sigh of relief when I came home and found my flat in solitude; perhaps it was the same solitude that now drove me into this place. I knew that I had loved Sabina for a while, but it disappeared in the pomp and pretension that the expectation of love propagates. And now after two years of sleeping with Anežka, I knew it was not love that drove me toward her. But I had cried at her bosom, I had held her dozens of times, even laughed with her (when I still knew how). Perhaps all I wanted were the eyes of a woman to look upon me and know that here I still stood. I raised my glass and swallowed the last of the brandy. Then I rose from my table, and taking my coat and hat, stepped out of the lounge and turned down the hall toward her room.

Standing outside her door I heard a beastly grunting and quiet cries. A fury ignited in me and without a thought I burst through the door and fell into the room. There on the bed on all fours was Anežka, dressed in some perverse garment. A fat man covered in patchy black hair stood behind her, thrusting violently. Her face was blue and black. Her right eye was so swollen that I wondered if she could see me. But she did see me. Her expression changed from shame to relief to horror and back again. The beast behind her looked at me and growled. He pushed Anežka away and jumped over the bed, lunging at me with his fist. He was drunk. I stepped out of the way and he crashed into the armoire. As he turned and tried to regain his balance I struck him in the stomach, and as he doubled over to hold his sore fatness, I struck him on his left cheek. He fell sideways toward the dresser, his cock still erect, his balls dangling, hair in thatches and lines all over his body. He was the ugliest creature I had ever seen. The thought of his hands groping Anežka, making her wear such obscene attire, beating her, and strangling her while he fucked her released an uncontrollable rage. As he kneeled before me, dull-eyed and foul, I took the lamp that sat on Anežka's dresser and smashed it over his head. He fell to the ground in a thump and I hoped him dead.

I went to the bed where Anežka lay weeping. On her neck were bruises so prominent that I could make out the length and width of each of the ugly man's fingers. Gentle lest I send her into hysterics, I laid my coat over her and picked her up in my arms. She did not resist; she only wept. Without any thought to where I was going, I held her close to me and carried her down the empty hallway to a small wooden door at the end. I pulled the latch and slipped into the back alley. With Anežka wrapped in my arms, I ran up the alley and into the dark street.

Shortly after we left the lounge, Anežka had stopped weeping, but still she stayed in my arms, neither of us objecting, neither of us speaking. She rested there (an uncomfortable position for her I would imagine) and stared out into the darkness of the street. Beneath her battered face was the story of a deeper wound, a wound that can only be inflicted by oneself. It was the pain of regret, of failed dreams and expectations, of a childhood completely lost. I could no longer remember being a child, and what had seen in Anežka was the same despairing realization. The world is crueller and far less forgiving than one ever thought possible.

I had to wake Anežka because I could not carry her up the stairs. I am not a strong man and so I was surprised that I had been able to carry her for as long as I did. My arms ached as I released her, but as we made our way up the stairs I held her as she took each step one at a time. Though not a word had been spoken between us and I knew it was terribly selfish, a part of me wished the staircase would go on forever, that one day we would find it ascended to the heavens.

We entered my flat and I closed the door behind us. I went to draw a bath and when I returned, Anežka was at the open window staring at the vista of Prague, this city that we both loved and despised. I came up behind her and silently we watched. As the minutes went on I could hear her breath catch, and soon tears fell from her eyes. I was hesitant to raise my hands and comfort her and so I stood, near but never touching, awkward and uncertain. The city below spoke to her, whether in consolation or in indifference. Anežka seemed to pour her misery out onto the steeples and saints, and what had begun as a whimper grew into weeping moans. She fell on her knees and so I sank to mine and hoped I could catch her. But as I wrapped my arms around her, she returned to the realities of life among men. She rose and began to wipe the tears from her face. She turned to me and apologized and I could not help but stare at the bruises on her neck and the deepening silver that swelled about her eye. A silence grew between us, and though before I had found it comfortable, I felt an indictment grow in my ears, and it was not from Anežka, but rather it was the reflection of myself in her.

From the bathroom I could hear that the bath was almost full and so I turned and fetched a towel. She took it from me with whispered thanks and then disappeared into the bathroom. I found a clean pair of pyjamas for her and laid out new sheets on the bed. They were crisp and smelled of soap and sun, and I breathed them in, hoping that Anežka would find some comfort in these miniscule pleasures. As I waited for her to emerge from the bath I stared out the window and smoked a cigarette. How strange that only this morning a breeze swept through this window and brushed my face, and now Anežka was in my apartment and I had beaten a man, perhaps even killed him. The thought amused me somehow, not the specific event, but the day's progression. Had the host of the bistro not sat me where he had I would not have viewed the amorous couple. Had I not viewed the amorous couple I would not have felt the compulsion to see Anežka, and then certainly I would have found myself alone in this apartment lingering over a bottle of brandy bemoaning the name of Petr Ludek. Petr Ludek. The name had barely crossed my mind all day, admonishments and condemnations had been kept at bay, replaced by the better, kinder, gentler Anežka. Had I believed in providence and fate, I would have certainly ascribed their work to this day.

My thoughts were halted by Anežka exiting the bathroom and I jumped to put out my cigarette. My bathrobe dangled over her small body, and she looked lost in it. I tried to smile empathetically at her, uncertain what to say that would make her more comfortable, more safe. Then she slipped the robe off and stood naked in my living room. I realized I had not yet thought of sleeping with her, yet here she offered herself as though in payment for my aid. A cool wind blew in from the window and she shivered. There was a sad beauty that emanated from her and I felt myself drawn to this sadness more than to any other part of her. I wanted to know why it was there, why she wore it so. I turned and picked up the pyjamas I had left for her on the bed and handed them to her.

"You can sleep on the bed. The floor will be fine for me." I smiled, at myself more so than at Anežka. She took the pyjamas and turned to slip into them. As though I were a gentleman, I turned my back to her to provide her with the illusion of privacy. I was acting a fool, I thought; immature to be sure. What would Anežka think of me when the sun rose the next morning? Childish or gallant? The sound of the bed creaking signalled that Anežka was pulling the covers about her. I moved and took a blanket from the trunk that sat against the bed and then walked near my desk on the far side of the room and spread it out on the floor.

With no words I could think of to comfort her, I said goodnight and turned off the lamp.

A few moments later, I heard Anežka whisper through the darkness. "Closer." She cleared her throat as though to navigate through the tears and then whispered again, "Please, come closer."

I walked over and laid the blanket out over the floor beside the bed. Then I lay down on the blanket, with each wooden floorboard claiming their individuality in my back. As my eyes adjusted to the dark, I saw Anežka's bruised hand dangling over the side of the bed. It was open as if to be held. I lifted my hand and slid my fingers through hers.

"Thank you," she whispered.

When I woke in the morning, Anežka was still asleep. Against every desire I rose and dressed for work. As Anežka slept on the bed, I watched her every breath; her cheek, which had turned a bluish silver, her hand, that I had clasped for as long as consciousness permitted, her hair, flowing over the pillow like moss might roll over stones in a deep forest. Never had she looked so beautiful. I leaned over her and kissed her head, smelling her hair; the soft lingering scent of soap and sun. I could not imagine, nor wanted to, what kind of evil would subject beautiful Anežka to lechery and perversion, conveniently stopping my thoughts from indicting myself. I did not want to fill this moment with my incessant ponderings and reflections, so I devoted all my senses to her.

As I walked out the door she still lay sleeping. I hoped that her mind was in the midst of the happy embrace of childhood dreams and waves of all she thought to be good. I looked back at her and felt that I had not cared so for a person for a very long time, though I could not help but think that I did not know her. Her likes and dislikes. Her joys and sorrows. I could not describe to you what she deemed good and what evil. Prescriptions and opinions on everything from Russians to horticulture, from rain to statues. I knew none of this, and yet I knew that part of me loved her and wished her to stay in my flat forever. And yet another part, a better part, knew that I had committed wrong against her and that goodness continued to elude me, despite the intoxicating invention of my night as deliverer and protector.

As I sat down at my desk, the entire weekend seemed like a distant memory or a dream that had never really happened. I had barely thought of Petr Ludek, barely condemned him, never mocked him. And I could not deny that now as I did think of him I did not feel the need to reproach him, nor did I feel the need to extol those convictions which now I hardly remembered. Toward Petr Ludek I felt nothing but a kind of fraternal affinity. I could not say why, but simply that hating him did not seem particularly important at the moment. And I wondered why it was that I had ever felt such hatred for him. Petr, just as the butcher and his German wife, just as

Ludmilla, and the student and the hundreds of others; just as Maminka and the priest and the weeping bureaucrat; and just as Anežka: all held a desire to live fully and unrestricted by the false convictions of state and society. To hold their dreams and childhood anticipations up to the world without having them torn down, sneered at, or condemned. I sat in my office aware of this simple assertion and its elementary liberalism. It was not that I had never thought of such a proposition, but rather that I did not care to refute it now. All I wanted was to be in my flat with Anežka in my arms. I sat at my desk with papers before me, but my mind was in my apartment, consumed with Anežka. Though it was not only Anežka that pressed upon me, it was the sun that had fallen on my face while sitting at the river, it was Maminka, it was Lady Zuza and Mrs. Vrbecová, it was the sincerity of the priest, it was my new affection for Petr Ludek and Zdeňa Havlová. I looked out the window at the grey apartment buildings as they sat in the sun. Between two of them hung a laundry line—brightly coloured bed sheets and clothes that danced and played in the waves of wind. I sat at my desk, watching the scene. Even here, in these anonymous buildings, life existed. I felt as though I was looking at a bright flower that had grown between the slabs of a sidewalk. The flower seems almost surprised at its own abilities, its tenacity to hope and grow. It is a perseverance of existence. And here I felt as though I was one of the buildings, unexpectedly stepping into the foreground, bright colours emanating from what I had thought was lifeless and grey.

My thoughts were disrupted by Jitka barging into my office, holding a new stack of papers. She put them down on my desk, appraised me and scowled at my daydreaming. She turned and slammed the door to my office. I heard the squealing of her chair as she pulled it from her desk and sat back down. I looked away from the window and began to sift through the papers. Warrant upon warrant upon warrant piled in front me. My heart sank and I felt the echo of virtue chased away, as night chases the day. I turned to the buildings, expecting the laundry to have been pulled in and clouds to have come over. But the sun still shone brightly in the cloudless sky, the laundry still fluttered and waved, and the world was still beautiful. I left the pile of names on the desk and spent the remainder of the morning staring out the window, as if to imprint into my memory the scene I knew would escape me forever once I filled out the warrants.

At lunchtime I ran into the street and took the streetcar all the way back to my apartment. The same urge that had caused me to look out at the buildings all morning propelled me to run to see Anežka, hoping to find her asleep in my bed, under the crisp sheets, with the bells ringing and the warm breeze caressing her face. But when I arrived at the apartment it was empty. She had neatly made the bed and folded my pyjamas and robe onto the pillow. Anger charged me and I swore, but I knew that what I had expected was unreasonable. I had thought that Anežka would leave her life and come live up here in my tower that looked over Prague. As my anger was replaced by disappointment and sadness, I sat on the bed. Folded on the pillow was a note. I opened it and read:

Thank you. You are a good man.

I read the single line over and over again, part of me baffled as to who she could mean, part of me sad that she had left, part of me rejoicing that she should think me good. And then as I read the note again, I thought of the pile of names and warrants that sat on my desk and I began to weep.

PART TWO

CLARITY IS A FUNNY THING. It can drop in on you without announcement, or it can grow within you, prolonging a sluggish introduction until it is revealed as a persistent stalker. But in either encounter, a meeting with clarity leaves you with an emerging sense of doubt. You cannot help but question if it really is a glimpse into a deeper truth, or if it is only a fleeting moment of inane weakness and zealous imagination. So it seems that clarity cannot exist alone. Faith must bolster it and hold it up, feed its truth and cherish its prophecies. Only then will clarity mean anything at all. Without faith, clarity would be as fickle and dismissible as any of the thousands of thoughts and ideas that pass over you and disappear into oblivion

I return to the office late from my lunch break, red-eyed and out of breath. Jitka sends a disapproving glare in my direction and taps her watch to indicate the time. I don't pretend to make excuses but simply disregard her and head for my office. At my desk, I stare at the pile before me. I stare at the papers and warrants, and then stare out the window. The bright-coloured laundry still floats gently in the breeze, still basks in the sun. I stare at the pile of names and warrants of people that will be ripped from this place and made to be forgotten. I think of the note left by Anežka and my heart beats louder and faster. Before me stand the butcher and his German wife. They no longer laugh; they know as well as I that I can no longer hide behind cynical proclamations and false convictions. Before me stand Mrs. Vrbecová and Lady Zuza, before me stand Maminka and the priest, Petr Ludek and Zdeňa, and all the names that have been seared into my brain. And in front of them all stands Anežka, sad eyed and beaten, but in glorious beauty. I cannot type. My fingers are numb, my arms are frozen, my mind too light to be weighed down by such darkness. All this because I fetched Lady Zuza out of the garbage chute, because Maminka had held me, because I had helped to pull Anežka from darkness, and because the sun had shone on my face and for a moment I made a choice to think the world good.

Outside my office sits Jitka Navratilová. She is the kind of person who is irked by any number of people and things: a change of breeze, a misplaced adjective, a wandering eye. Not long ago, I watched as for half an hour she chased a fly around her desk, furiously dancing and slapping her hand against the wall, the desk, the window, even going so far as to hurl a book across the room at it, succeeding only in knocking over a pile of papers. The fly still buzzed around her (undoubtedly revelling in it) as Jitka groaned obscenities and strained to pick up the fallen papers. The fly flew into my office through the crack in the door from where I had been watching. I lit a cigarette and smoked while the fly ran himself repetitively into the windowpane. He bounced against the glass in vain, trying to reach the freedom on the other side. When I arrived at work the following day, the fly lay dead on the windowsill. The day before, I easily could have opened the window and let him escape, but I could not have cared less. So now, I cannot help but wonder: was my apathy toward the fly any different than Jitka's exertions? The product—a dead fly—was the end result of either intention. To the fly beating itself against the window, pleading for escape, Jitka Navratilová and I were the same. And so it has been the case for a long time. I have formulated judgments and dispensed them to everyone but me. To Petr Ludek, to the State, to Jitka, to the men of the lounge, to Maminka, and even to Anežka. Yet what of myself? Dare I pass judgment upon myself, irrespective of intention? Dare I judge only on action, only on the creation or destruction of my own hands? What will the gods determine as my fate? How will Petr Ludek and the list of names, how will Anežka, how shall I judge what I am?

I begin to type, and just as my fingers had been used before to erase the names of dozens, now they jump from key to key to remember them. And each name that was imprinted into my memory, each spouse, each child, each occupation, and each offence comes crashing down on page after page. I see them all as they stand before me and their spirits suffuse every sheet of paper. It is a revocation of their sentence, a revocation of my own sentence. And as the sun casts a shadow over the waving laundry, I take the completed pile of names and slide it under my shirt. Then I run to my apartment in a reckless sprint.

I WAVE A GREETING TO MRS. VRBECOVÁ who sits by the door holding a broom in her hand and Lady Zuza in her lap. I run up the stairs and, once in my flat, lock the door behind me. The air is laced with a curious anticipation, as though invisible fireworks are exploding silently all around me. I pull from under my shirt the list of names and set them on the bed beside Anežka's note. Then I loosen my tie, slip out of my shirt and pants and walk up to the window. The last rays of the sun fall over the red roofs and steeples and towers of this city which I hate and love. The golden sunbeams fall over my naked body and purify me. Down in the streets below people walk back and forth, never looking up, only straight ahead. They do not see the saints looking down on them, and at this moment I join the saints in looking down at this city and its confused throngs. I close my eyes and let this baptism momentarily wash away the deeds which I committed and my apathy hid. The eyes of the world bathe me in a graceful light and I feel myself elevated, as though a caucus of goodness that had once proclaimed me lost now revokes its judgment and intercedes to the gods for my salvation.

When the sun has set, I go to my bed and take the pile of names and Anežka's note and I sit on the floor. Placing the note on the dusty floorboards, I begin to spread the typed list around it, putting each in its place, each name seared into my memory, each name that cannot be forgotten. When I am finished, the pages cover the floor. They surround and swarm Anežka's note, each page an overwhelming argument against my goodness. Here in the darkness I stare at the names that surround me, these that I condemned because I was told to condemn, because I was afraid and hid my fear behind a curtain of cynicism and apathy. I fall on the names and begin to weep. In the cold darkness of my apartment I weep over them and beg for their forgiveness.

—

I AWAKE PLANTED ON THE NAMES. Dawn has not yet broken the sky and the deep blue of a diminishing darkness fills my room. I am shivering and so rise and crawl into the tub. The pipes rumble and vibrate and my whole body is attacked by the cold water that bursts from the showerhead and drives the sleep from my eyes. As the water warms, I think of the names that cover my flat and the zeal which prompted me to so frantically write them, the fervour of my run home, my baptism in the rays of the sun, and my supplication for forgiveness. And though I feel a kind of ignited passion, sadness looms over me because I know what must be done. I am afraid, because knowing that goodness exists is not enough. One must enact goodness if one can claim it. So I sit in the shower with the growing resignation that I can no longer remain an anonymous part of the background.

I sit at my desk all morning and stare out into nothing. Occasionally I flip through the latest pile of names and warrants. Every so often, my fingers sporadically jump along the typewriter keys at random, spelling out gibberish for the benefit of Jitka's prying ears. But I can write nothing of substance, no word that can be read or spoken. I am afraid to act, and afraid not to act. To reclaim my laughter, yet lose my life. And so a battle of fates rages on. Rationales to fill the warrants and sign my name hold siege over my mind, and yet to my surprise the rationales cannot penetrate the walls of my new determination. I cannot continue to create hatred for these names, even if my survival demands it. Beyond apathy or indifference, hatred is the only possible rationale for my actions, but I am exhausted by hate and my perpetual justifications, for the hatred itself is irrational. If I ignore reason and continue to feed on hatred and indifference, then I will have cause to tremble. For the saints do not take pity on convenient self-delusions. Self preservation and self interest are not arguments for virtue.

Although I have idly flipped through the latest pile of names, I have not read it. I have not read the names for which I will condemn myself; whether I speak out or complete the warrants, I am caught in a double bind. On one hand I could complete the warrants, and go on as I have, though the last few weeks stand as strong arguments against such a choice. On the other, I could refuse to complete the warrants and then face the prosecution of the State. There is no escape; in either direction my existence is threatened. And so I must once again ask the question I asked some time ago: why does Petr Ludek speak out against power when there is so little hope of success? The answer is dishearteningly simple: because he chooses to. Bolstered by a clarity of purpose, and a faith in goodness, Petr is compelled to act.

THE PILE OF NAMES SITS MONOLITHICALLY ON MY DESK. With masochistic indulgence I flip through the pages again, my eyes half reading, half intoxicated by what sits before me. And then there is a name of a church that catches my scanning vision:

```
Kohout, Václav
d.o.b: May 1, 1906
Saint Pravoslav, Prague
Children - None
Spouse - None
Roman Catholic Priest
Counter-revolutionary activities.
```

I dare guess that it is the priest with whom I spoke. I remember our conversation and think of all he told me, but also what I told him. He did not stand between the pews and judge me; he did not condemn me. And yet now he is listed. It seems strange to place a real face to a name, not one conjured by the lamenting imagination of my guilty conscience, but a real person who will suffer through this in all the pain and horror that comes with flesh and blood.

At lunchtime I jump on a streetcar and make my way across the bridge. The sun is out again, harshly defining the lines between shade and light. I make my way through the streets, trying to remember the path I took to the church only a few days ago. After a number of false turns I once again find myself in front of the imposing faces of saints carved into the walls and door. Towering before me, the church stands before me as a temptation to stray from Party lines. It is different to enter now than it was under the cover of darkness. There is a very good chance that this church is being watched by eyes hidden in some dark corner, waiting to write down my name. I cannot go further. My zeal has faltered and fear prohibits me from entering. I look about me and then turn and walk away as quickly as I came.

I slip into a boisterous pub a little way down the road from the church. I sit in front of the window and stare out, trying to find the eyes that bore into my back, but I see nothing. My paranoia is interrupted by the waiter, and I order a beer so I will melt into the background as I melt my fears. He returns with it promptly and I stare back out onto the street. I am convinced there are eyes that lurk beyond the glass, though my reason cannot prove it. I gulp down my beer and pay. I feel light headed and realize that I have not eaten for some time. The beer has eased my mistrust of the street and so I dare to venture out into the shadows of Saint Pravoslav. A woman selling bread stands across from the church entrance and I make my way over to her. I take my time searching for change, asking her about the weather, but she does not address my questions with any interest. I linger as I eat my bread, half engaged in banal discussion with the woman, half watching the church. As I stand there, the door opens and I see the small figure of the priest. Underneath the saints and columns he looks remarkably small. His dwarfed figure makes its way down the front steps and into the street. He walks as though he is free, or rather that he believes he is free, his deliberate pace a defiance of his pending sentence. As I watch him, the old woman selling the bread disappears into the background noise of the street, people coming and going, moving like snakes around a blind mouse. I make my way after him, walking no faster than he, watching his every bounce, his every greeting. I am following him and I do not know why. I have no intention of going up to him and describing to him my position and my sudden salvation. To tap his shoulder and speak to him face to face, to explain myself; what vanity! What righteousness I could claim! I imagine my reflection in his eyes and the tone of my confession; affirmed salvation and granted kingdom. I could not bear it, I do not want him to know it is I, as though his prayers for my soul, or the whispered words in a dark church broke my Party allegiance and I transfigured into a penitent Christian.

I see a little boy, no more than eight years old, carrying a package in the street. I move toward him. I expect, or rather hope, that he is too young to know of the evils of Communists or priests or bureaucrats. "Hello there," I say. He looks up at me without saying a word and I feel the awkwardness that I always feel when around children. "I see a friend of mine, down the street. He's wearing all black—see?" I point in the direction of the priest and spot his black garb between the moving colours of people. The boy nods. "I'd like you to give him a note for me. Can you do that?" The boy nods his head and I pat his shoulder, but my hand betrays my unfamiliarity with children and proves that I never have had, nor should have had them. I take out a pen and paper and write out in messy haste:

Leave the country. A warrant will be out for your arrest.
– A friend from the darkness

I hesitate with this signature, but know that, for all my desire to remain anonymous, it will prove to him that this is not a trick. That this comes from that lost and cynical man. I hand it to the boy and urge him to run after the priest. He dashes off without a word before I can slip a crown into his pocket. I watch, hidden in a building's entranceway, as the boy steers between the moving people. Upon reaching him, the boy tugs on the priest's black shirt. He turns, surprised by the child at his feet. The boy holds out the note and the priest takes it, then the boy dashes off, disappearing into the crowd. As I watch him read the note, I can feel my heart beating and my temples pulsating as blood rushes to every limb, pumped by this ethereal zeal of goodness. The priest looks around and I slide behind the outcropping of the heavy entranceway. I wait a moment and then cautiously peek back into the street. The priest still stands where he was, and around him flutter the torn remnants of my note. Shredded by his hands, the crumbs of my first act of goodness are taken by the wind and sweep toward me like scorned sinners fleeing the holy. They blow past me, tumbling over the cobblestones of the street. I think of my sentimental reverence for Anežka's note and though I did not expect it, I had hoped the priest would have held my note a little longer. Goodness, it seems, is not exclusive of vanity.

The priest resumes his stroll as though he has escaped an unpleasant encounter. I turn and walk in the opposite direction, past the woman selling bread, past the church and back to the streetcar. I notice nothing on my return trip, my mind fuelled by the image of the priest walking off into the distance and into the shackles of the State. Perhaps he is resigned to stay in his homeland. Perhaps he feels that times will change soon enough. Or perhaps he believes that to run is to acquiesce. I do not know and I will never know. The priest will join the thousands of names that have already been laid out to disappear. And I wonder if the day is not so far away when my name will join his.

Living Among the Dead

I wait for Jitka to leave for the day and then take the pile of warrants and new list of names and slide them under my shirt. I arrive home and immediately sit down at my desk, pulling out the papers. They are damp with sweat; I am not impervious to fear, it seems. I lay them down beside my typewriter and step into the washroom. My stomach is in knots; my body is covered in sweat, and every limb quivers and trembles in fear. I cannot remember why I chose this for myself, and yet fear has not stopped me. I take off my shirt and wash my face. The water is refreshing and it soothes my agitated brain. I look in the mirror. It has been so long since I have looked into my own eyes for fear of what I would find, but here I look, here I search. There is nothing astonishing, and yet I am astonished. There is nothing specific to take note of, and yet here I stand unable to look away, for what I see is the whisper of laughter. It is not the mocking laughter of the cinema. It is an echo of what sits in Petr Ludek's eyes, or the butcher's, or his German wife. It is the faint laughter of humanity.

Encouraged by what I have seen, I sit back down at my desk. I look at the new list of names. It is only a series of rows and columns: name, date of birth, occupation, spouse, children, offence. It will not be so difficult to copy. I pull out the supplies I have stolen from the office and begin to mark out hundreds of lines for the dozens of rows and columns that will house the names of those that do not exist except in my memory and imagination.

I scroll through my address book, writing down the names of people I know have either emigrated or died. I run out of names much sooner than I expected. I rise from the table and impatiently pour myself a drink. Then I grab a pad of paper and a pen, slide into my coat and step out into the slumbering evening light.

It takes me much longer than I anticipated to reach the cemetery. Taking two streetcars, a bus, and then walking several blocks, I arrive when night is already heavy upon the city. I hop the fence to avoid any queries from the caretaker and carefully manoeuvre between the tombstones and graves of the long deceased. Adrenaline is rushing through me. I have no apprehensions of spirits or ghosts, and I barely pay attention to the clapping poplars above that would, in other circumstances, create a frightening scene. But all that frightens me now is the secret police. I would rather confront the most frustrated of ghosts if it meant I would never have to see the face of a police officer. I walk until I am in the darkness, far away from the glowing lights of the caretaker's cabin. I take out my pen and paper and begin to make a new list, looking for tombstones that contain more information than just the date of birth and death, and am surprised to find many include the names of spouses, places of birth, names of children, even professions. The more written about the dead, the less likely that an innocent should be taken. Even so, are we all not innocents under this oppression?

In the moonlight I can see without a light but as a cloud passes over me there is darkness and the stones disappear into the shadows. I sit and wait for the moon to return but the cloud is large, and I grow afraid. After glancing back at the caretaker's hut, I take out my lighter to illuminate the tombstones and continue writing down the names. As I flip the pad to the third page and frantically scribble down Stanislav Vaček, my shadow is suddenly cast on the stone and a trembling voice cries out, "Who's there?" I fall onto the ground, ducking out of the light. My body trembles with anxiety, and I crawl between the tombstones. I slither like a clumsy snake between graves, excusing myself to the bodies that lie six feet beneath me. In one hand I clutch the pad of paper, in the other the pen. It seems my frantic scrambling terrifies the caretaker, and he stays away, calling out into the darkness to reveal myself, lest I be a spirit. I almost laugh at this, but my laughter is stopped when I come upon a hill rather suddenly and roll down, landing against a tombstone. As I turn and cradle my injured shoulder, I hear the caretaker cry out from the other side of the hill, "Be you spirit or man, show yourself!" I fight the urge to call out "spirit" and burst into a fit of laughter. Soon the dim shadows that appeared at the top of the hill disappear and in the distance I hear the caretaker grumbling and the creaking sound of the door closing. Still, I lie and wait for some time. The moon, hidden for a moment behind another cloud, allows for patches of stars to penetrate between the cover. They twinkle and look down upon me. These tiny specks of light, like sparkling sand sprinkled over black velvet, have shone for an eternity. They have shone over kings, popes, and bishops. Over communists, fascists, and republicans. Over Czechs, Slovaks, Germans, and Russians. And yet, through it all, the one constant has been the human person. Stripped of ideology, religion, title or nationality, every person on this globe has stood under the stars, no closer, no farther. Every person has had to turn their neck and look up, and this thought contents me.

The moon once again shows itself and I stand, my shoulder still sore. I search for the pad which I lost on my whirl down the hill and soon find it. I turn around. Before me, row on row, are the graves laid out by the State. These are not the graves of the intended forgotten, but line upon line of men slaughtered in battle, those who gave their life for a country now occupied by others. For what did they give it? I wish I could say that as I stand among these graves a wave of patriotic pride comes over me, but all I feel is an incredible sadness. It is the sadness of waste, of spoiled lives, of lives deceived to fight for a cause that was created by men who sit at desks far away from danger. And now the ground beneath me is filled with the deceived dead, rotting in the cold earth. The men who sit in comfortable chairs call this "sacrifice," but what do they know of sacrifice? They wave banners of freedom and liberty as they invade and oppress. They ignore the will of the people just as they proclaim that they are its fulfillment. I begin to write each name as though it is a vindication against the State which killed them. Not the Russian state, or the Czechoslovak Republic, or the Nazi state. But the State: that false thing set out by the powerful to entrench themselves against those they proclaim to serve. East or West, North or South, it does not matter. Old men will always send the young to die. Standing in this place, there is nothing but venom in my body for this institution that has caused misery for so many. Caused families to separate, to flee, to fight, to kill. And for what? Leaders cry freedom, liberty, and democracy. They proclaim that they are the will of the people and yet it is the will of the people that terrifies them above all. Make no mistake, it is in the West as it is here. Here our will is bent to the Party, but in the West, will is bent to those that pay one's wage. I do not resist here to become like the West. I resist here because now, at this moment, goodness requires no less.

Here I stand, and I profess that from this moment on, I will not do the work of any master who bears the word of state, whether East or West, North, or South. Those who suppress, those who do violence, those who kill and send the young to be killed. Those who plot to destroy the will of the people, those who ignore it, those who leave men and women on the street to beg for their food, those who make secret arrests, those who listen to our conversations and make us to be afraid, those who steal food from our mouths and use it to fatten their bellies, those who call upon liberty and freedom when they mean oppression and submission, those who use their power to exploit the powerless. Here in this place, I kneel down before these men who lie six feet below me. There is nothing moving or spiritual about it. It sickens me, and as I kneel, I swear to their spirits never will I take up the sword, or the pen, the fist, or the hammer in pursuit of the State, to help prop up the powerful. And I swear that I will be their vindication.

THE NEXT MORNING, I sit at my desk with my head falling to my chest and my eyes closing. All I want is to sleep. In front of me sits a pile of completed warrants and a list of names that should be identical to the one given to me by Jitka, and yet they have nothing in common but their appearance. Jitka's is the list of the condemned living, mine is the list of vindication.

The past night, I missed the last bus, and then the last streetcar and so was forced to rely upon my legs. I arrived at my apartment just as dawn cracked the sky. I lay down, but could not sleep. A vision of the decaying bodies of men abused by the State occupied my mind. So I rose and began to fill out the warrants, sixty-four in all. When I finished, each one was listed with the name of a perished soldier, a man betrayed and shot down by the State. At long last, these soldiers had become true protectors of the people, true guardians of liberty and freedom.

With a despairing sigh, I take the papers in hand. The walk to Jitka's desk has never seemed so short. I had expected a delay, a small procession to rethink things and turn around, or to gain complete confidence in my actions. But neither comes to me and I find myself hovering over Jitka's desk, and her peering eyes and paranoid scowl, much too quickly. She asks if I have finished the papers (she does not use the word warrants); I nod but do not hand them to her. With a sneer, she says she is surprised I have completed the task so quickly, because it took me almost the whole of last week to complete just as many.

To this I cannot resist replying, "Jitka, my dear woman, my dedication and passion for the cause grows."

She doesn't answer and what is on her face is more than scorn; it is a kind of repugnance. If I were not so tired, I think I would laugh at her. She extends her hand for the papers. I stare at them for a moment, then exhale, place them in her hand and walk away. My tribute to the fallen has been completed, and in a few days, perhaps a week, my life will be over.

Sitting at my desk, I lean back in my chair. The moment has faded and yet its repercussions hang about me with intensity. This is it. I have leapt from perpetrator to subversive in a single, irreversible act. I have given up all for this cause. They will find me quickly, and when they do, they will take me away. They will imprison me. They will beat me. Perhaps they will kill me. And what will Jitka say to my replacement? Perhaps she will tell him just what she told me: that one day, he simply did not come into work.

Wistful Projections

When I fell in love the first time, I was perhaps ten or eleven years old. Zlatá Hruškova had round cheeks and always wore yellow ribbons in her dark hair. I have vague memories of endless giggles and awkward hand holding. Other than that, I can hardly remember her, except for one memory which I can recall with the same vividness as if it happened yesterday. It was spring, perhaps in March or April. A warm rain was falling heavily from the sky, and Zlatá and I huddled in a small abandoned lean-to on a forest path near my home. The smell of the wet earth and wet trees filled the air. Creaking pines breathed a tangible sigh of relief at winter's end, while naked oaks and maples impatiently drank each raindrop to embolden their buds to break forth into leaf. Rainwater ran off the roof of the shelter and into a makeshift gutter that then poured it forth in a gushing waterfall onto the forest floor. Zlatá and I lay on the damp hay in the lean-to, listening to the rain, and watching the water cascade from the roof to the ground. She stood up, and taking my hand in hers, led me to the moving water. With a melodic laugh, she brought her head from under the shelter and into the flowing stream of rainwater from the gutter. The water ran over her head, and she giggled, putting her hands over her ears. She motioned for me to do the same, and so I hesitantly followed suit and stuck my head under the stream and covered my ears with my hands. As the water ran between my ears and hands, it sealed them from sound and all I could hear was my inner self. It was the sound of my heart beating. It was the sound of blood rushing through my body. It was the sound of water hitting my head and running over my face. It was the taste of the water—fresh and pure. It was the smell of the forest, of stretched-out pines and basking maples. It was the bliss I saw in Zlatá's expression; the utter joy of existing in no moment but the present. Void of past, and irrespective of the future. And I was the same. Without a past, I was innocent and irreproachable. I remember looking at her and thinking, "This is what love is like, this is what life is like."

But we age, and innocence is chased away by proclamations of maturity. And so we cling to that singular moment of perfection continuously trying to reclaim it. Whether it is our first love or not, we pursue it, try to evoke it, create it, pretend it, but with each attempt it is driven further away from us. It is like a fresh step in a dew-covered meadow, or in the virgin sand of an untouched beach. Once you walk through it, it is never the same; the march can never be undone. Like the moment with Zlatá in the forest, like first love, like childhood; it is lived only once, then lost.

I sit in a café and wait for Anežka. It has been two days since my visit to the cemetery and Jitka has not delivered any new lists or empty warrants to my desk. As I sit here sipping my coffee and watching people go by, I know my days are numbered. I am surprised by how calm I am at the thought of being arrested, erased, and forgotten. Having spent years working for the Party, I know that if it is efficient at one thing, it is in hunting down and prosecuting its enemies. I do not feel as though I am its enemy, but I know they believe I am. The Party will of course be further incensed that a comrade, one of their own, has so betrayed their trust, and the great malleable "will of the people" will hunt me down with ferocity. They will make no sparing sentence or grant a merciful reprieve. They will punish me as severely as their veneer of morality and "justice" will allow. I know this better than most. Such is the misfortune of being a trusted Party bureaucrat.

I look at my watch and see that Anežka is late. I wonder if perhaps she will not come. Over the last few days, I left several messages for her at the lounge. I eagerly waited for a reply, but she only responded to me today, and when I asked if she would meet me for coffee, she agreed, reluctantly I think. So now I sit here, excited and foolish. What can I possibly expect from her? After two years, I wonder what she really thinks of me. Shall I dare cast myself as a friend, or even more audaciously, a lover? Yet anything less would cause me grief. I recognize the absurdity of such longing, and I can feel the underlying grimace within me: such a hope is superfluous and full of folly. What are these ivory-tower expectations that plague us and cause us to falter? They propel us to act against reason in an effort to satiate our vacuous desires, and then lament their failure.

And what of the expectations that we are held up to? We walk in the directions directed by the State, society, friends, family, and lovers. To be strapped with the weights of Party fealty, familial loyalty, or a lover's fidelity. I cannot deny that it is oppressive, but neither can I deny that it is also fundamental to our nature. To be so intrinsic to the fabric of those around us; to be held in esteem; to be desired; to be welcomed into the paradise of one's kin. One could hardly be forgotten, or made to disappear. To be incorporated into Anežka's dreams of paradise; what a strange thought. Yet isn't that what love is? To hope to share paradise with another—a lover, a friend. To pray to the saints to grant residence in the same haven. Is that not love? Did I not share a fraction of paradise with Zlatá in the forest rain? To step into memory with Anežka and hold up the walls of paradise long enough to have her stand in the warm rain and let the water wash over her face. To smile together into the face of creation, as we stand hand in hand.

It seems strange to not know more of Anežka, given our history. Years of company and our moments of physical intimacy, and yet there is very little that I know of her. And so it seems to me that this corresponds with the unfortunate situation that has existed since God created Eve from the rib of Adam. Eve has been relegated to the background and only brought forth when convenient for the man. I know that my experience with Anežka has reinforced such archetypes, and she has fallen into such a role. I do not know of Anežka's past, because she has never told me. I do not know why she spends her time at the lounge, entertaining Party officials. All I know is what I have learned from our mostly physical interactions, or from observing her, and so she remains a mystery. Perhaps Anežka keeps her past a secret because it is the only way she can hold onto it. Perhaps she does not say much because she is not paid to speak and so she retains this as her own. Powerful men have ordained the roles that women will be cast in—whore, comforter, nurturer—to suit their own needs. Anežka is caught in this brutal garden of men, so she holds to her profession as an unconscious hyperbole of the absurdity to which she has been relegated in the story of her life.

When Anežka does finally arrive, she sits across from me, a smile of greeting on her face. Around her neck she wears her emerald green shawl, which covers the finger-marks on her throat. Her eyes are eclipsed by dark glasses, but under them I can still see the black and blue of her beaten face. I want to ask her to take off her glasses but I do not. I enquire how she is, and she says she is fine and then thanks me again. She sounds embarrassed, as though I have seen her at her most vulnerable and now she wishes to keep her distance. She tells me that the man in her room was taken to the hospital, and only suffered a mild concussion.

"He didn't go to the police?" I ask.

"Of course not."

"So you've had no trouble from them?"

"None."

"And where are you staying?"

"At my apartment of course." She looks surprised.

"Yes, of course. And have you found employment? There is a position at my office—"

"Why should I be looking for new work? Do you think this is the first time something like this has happened?" A laugh escapes her as she smiles at me incredulously and I find myself unable to respond.

"But surely there must be some other work."

She remains silent.

"Surely work for someone such as yourself cannot be so hard to find."

Again she does not answer, and does not speak until the waiter arrives with her coffee and she thanks him. Then silence. She does not need me to understand, that is clear. Is she only here at my request and pathetic supplication? And yet she must have some affinity for me; why else would she be here? But as I gaze at her, I see a sadness inside her, the same sadness I saw the night she was beaten. It is similar to the sadness in Maminka's eyes—a lamentation for a lost past.

We sit for some time in silence, with little to say to one another, and yet in this silence I long for her. I want to look into her eyes and understand her. I offer her a cigarette and she accepts but makes no attempt at conversation. It is not the silence of coldness, nor the silence of trauma, but the silence of indifference. And I suddenly feel great embarrassment for having cried at her bosom or paid to have her in my bed.

"What is it?" she asks.

I pause momentarily, but sigh and divulge myself. "I am ashamed."

"You have been kind to me."

"I am sorry."

"You have no need to be sorry."

"You must think that I am one of them, like any other man in that place. But I am different. I am more."

She smiles at me and says, "You are a good man." And though I am happy at these words, her smile speaks more of pity than agreement that I am indeed different. She leans in and takes my hand in her own. And, as she holds my hand, I feel the shame inside me grow and the collective guilt of my sex fall upon me. I look at Anežka and I see a woman that has been designated to a life overrun by the abuses of my gender, the roles we have required her to play: of lover and nurturer, of saint and sinner. Men cry and expect to be comforted, men fuck, men love and expect returned affection, men decry her as whore and beat her, men claim her as saint and beat her. And yet she has survived and weaves between the atrocities inflicted upon her to build her own life, separate from mine and from anyone else. And this is why I do not really know who Anežka is. Her life is not dependent on mine or another man's; it is her own, to claim for her own, and to make known on her own.

We sit and she holds my hand, because she is compassionate and sees the sorrow in me, and again I long to know her. But soon she rises and bids me goodbye. Leaning over me she kisses my cheek, and then turns and leaves. I sit at the table. The sun is sinking and the street lights begin to glow and still I sit, mesmerized by the woman I love.

I watch through the window as she walks down the street, her grey coat melting into the lengthening shadows of dusk, her dark hair bouncing with each step. Each dissipating moment cries out with an urge to rise and chase after her, take her by the hand and lead her to that lean-to in the woods, where the rain falls in streams and the air smells of pine. All I can think as I watch her walk away is that today may be the last chance for me to pursue her, to make a proclamation of love, to make her see that I am different. Tomorrow I may find myself under arrest and locked away, forgotten by the world. The growing shadows mark the seconds like monuments to lost chances, and before I can debate it further I am on my feet and running through the crowd. I run blindly in the direction where I last saw her, my eyes frantically searching, and the sweat on my forehead grows each moment that I cannot see her. And there she is, on the other side of the open square, her emerald scarf undeniable. I sprint across the square and a flock of pigeons in the centre is disturbed by my gallop and launch into the air in a flurry of chatter and beating wings. In the moving air that surrounds me, I lose sight of her for only a moment before my eyes latch onto her once again. As I draw nearer, it comes to mind what I will say to her and what I expect her to say to me. And so I stumble and am abruptly frozen. What am I to her but another man who has proven the world to be harsh and impenetrable?

I watch her turn onto a small street and follow behind. The small street is in fact an alley and Anežka mounts a metallic staircase bolted to the side of a shabby building. I listen to the sound of her shoes against the metal steps and from my position behind the wall I see her standing before a decrepit green door. A last ray of sunlight peeks through the adjacent buildings and shines against the door beside her. With her keys in hand, she pauses for a moment and moves into the light. The orange glow imbues her face with a natural radiance. She removes her scarf, revealing the silver-blue bruises that encircle her neck, as if hoping that these rays will wash them away—or perhaps wash her away. And for a moment they do. The sun shines down upon her and she looks as if she were part of the light, translucent and incandescent. Then, just as quickly as they appeared, the orange rays of the dying sun fade, and her face rejoins the rest of the alley in the diminishing blue of dusk.

She looks down at the shawl, as though her moment with the sun was a foolish indulgence. Then she turns to the green door, unlocks it, pushes it open, and disappears behind it.

—

I REMAIN AT THE EDGE OF THE ALLEY, smoking a cigarette and waiting. I suppose I wait for a sudden surge of confidence or courage, but none comes. I take a long drag and wonder what I am doing here, what foolishness has brought me to stand at the bottom of Anežka's staircase. The muffled sounds of a record, playing the wail of a klezmer violin, fill the alley. The alley is draped in its regretful sob. I am terrified to walk up the stairs to the green door and knock. But I know that terror is easier to overcome than regret, and that this may be the last time I may ever speak or see Anežka, to make her see that I am more than a man soliciting sex in a state-run bordello. The police may be waiting at my flat, interrogating Mrs. Vrbecová as they prepare to arrest me. And so with the weeping violin propelling me, I throw my cigarette to the ground and mount the steps.

I knock on the green door, and a moment passes. The music continues, the sky grows darker, the alley colder. Then the door opens slightly and Anežka's beaten eye appears between the green of the door and the frame, betraying a kind of irritated surprise. "What are you doing here?"

I stutter and search for a reason besides the obvious but I can think of none, and so I ask her if I can come in.

"What do you want?"

I tell her that I just want to talk with her.

A moment passes, and she stands in the doorway appraising me. Then the door swings open and Anežka turns and steps back into the room. "If you want to come in, then come in," she says indulgently. Indeed, I remain at the door, like a nervous child. With a self-reproaching caution I step through the doorway and close the door behind me. The small room holds a sink and counter on the wall to my right. In the centre of the room sits a table, made of warped wooden planks haphazardly nailed together. The record player that continues to weep its sad fiddles and accordion sits in the far corner. And in the middle of a wall covered with cupboards and shelves is a window that looks out onto the street. My eyes pore over the room, not to judge, but to look into Anežka and discover her inner intricacies.

"Drink?" she asks.

"Please."

Anežka places two glasses on the table and fills them with vodka. She looks entirely changed from our earlier encounter. She is now wearing a loose shirt and worn pants, and she holds a cigarette in her right hand, elegantly bringing it to her lips in long intervals. I have never seen her so relaxed, and I am glad that she has this small flat at the end of an alley that she shares with no one but who she chooses. And because she has let the door open for me, I cannot help but smile. A pathetic, happy, adolescent smile.

She falls into a rickety wooden chair at the table, and I follow suit, taking a place across from her. "And what did you want to talk about?" she asks, taking the glass in hand.

"Anything," I say at last.

She laughs and it seems to erase the bruises around her eye and on her neck. "Well, I'm not much for talking about anything, or nothing, for that matter."

"I'd like to know about you. Who you are, where you came from, how came to live in Prague."

"Why do you want to know those things?" She looks unsettled, or perhaps annoyed. "Why after all this time?"

"Maybe because I've finally come to my senses."

"You had no need to ask before. And I have no need to divulge my soul." She pauses for a moment. "I don't mean to sound ungrateful, but that night I would have been all right. It's not the first time that something like that has happened, and it won't be the last." As she speaks I cannot help but feel entirely ridiculous for sitting here in her kitchen, asking her these things after I have spent so much time with her. Embarrassment and shame are lodged in each sip of vodka I take, and each word that is spoken. I feel like a little boy, supplicating to his childhood sweetheart. And when she finishes speaking I can only look at her and entirely agree, and so I tell her I am sorry for that night when I caused her pain.

She takes a sip of vodka and fans away my words with her hand. "There's no need for that."

"But there is. You deserve better than that. Than all of it."

"You're probably right."

"This world ought be a better place for you."

She looks at me, her brow furrowing, and I can feel her eyes appraising me. "You're different now."

I smile. "How so?"

"The way you look at me, the way you speak. You seem," she pauses as though is searching for the word, "awake."

"I suppose I am."

"What changed?"

"I don't know. Everything."

"That I can't believe."

"What do you mean?"

Anežka takes a long sip from her glass. "Because if everything changed, all that means really is that you changed. So what made you change?"

"I suppose you're right." I release a contented sigh and gaze at her. She is sitting across from me and I feel strangely intimidated by her. As if she could take each word of mine and laugh at it, mock it. And yet I trust she will not. "I rescued my landlady's cat."

"What?"

"I pulled my landlady's cat from the garbage chute."

"I don't understand."

"Perhaps," I pause, searching for an explanation. Can I really divulge the secret of the names? I tremble at the thought. "I don't know really," I say.

"Fair enough." She laughs and takes a long drag from her cigarette. "So what do you want to know about me?"

"Anything," I say, and then, afraid she may escape in the expanse of the question, ask, "Where is your mother? Your father?"

After a long sigh, she begins. "My mother is in Klašterec. My father is dead. He was a Jew, and my mother hid him from the Nazis for four years in the basement of her home. But when she became pregnant, whispers around town grew to accusations that there was someone else living with her, a Jew. In the last year of the war, just before I was born, the Nazis came for him, and..." She wavers and takes a drink. "Because my mother was Czech she lived, because my father was Jewish he died. I have often wondered how I fit between these worlds." She sighs and, taking a last drag from her cigarette, extinguishes it in the ashtray. She watches the weaving line of smoke meander from the tray and diffuse into the air. Then she turns her eyes to me again. "Is that what you were looking for?"

"What do you mean?"

"Tell me you didn't come here to discover why poor little Anežka became what she is. Why does she fuck these men for bonds and money when she could sit in an office and file papers, or sell newspapers? Isn't that why you came here?"

I do not answer, not because it is necessarily true, but because I cannot say it is untrue. In the light of Anežka's story, she is different; suddenly she is endowed with a past. Her story and history almost tangibly trail behind her.

She takes her drink in hand and swallows the rest. She refills her glass and fiddles through her case for a cigarette. She lights it and offers me one. I thank her and accept. She rises from the chair and moves to the record player, pulling the klezmer record off the turntable. "Any requests?" she asks.

"What do you have?"

She leafs through a pile of records and, choosing one, slides it from its cover and carefully places the needle onto its surface. Sound fills the air as Anežka returns to her chair. Violins grow in unison with the crescendo staccato of a trumpet. Soon Édith Piaf breaks forth in her determined anthem, "Non, Je Ne Regrette Rien." And I cannot help but smile that this is the record Anežka has chosen. She sees my smile, and her face reflects pleasure in my having noticed the irony of the choice. It is a song about regret, or rather the absence of it in what some may say is a life that ought be replete with it. And it seems to be a stronger evocation of ourselves than either one of use could ever express in words. Piaf's voice rises with the violins and brass with such lamentable ferocity that one cannot help but believe the words. We sit with silly expressions on our faces, and under her breath I can see Anežka whispering the words as though they were a canticle of her life.

The song finishes and, aside from the blotchy sounds from the record player, there is silence. Anežka and I look at each other and laugh—a velvet laugh that is full of comfort. To say that one has no regrets is simply to say that one has too many to keep count of, that the past is never forgotten or escaped. We are today what we chose to be yesterday. We are the unwilling historical participants of our own creations. We make choices today that tomorrow we will wish we had not made. And so we laugh, because if we did not we would weep. And as our laughter fills the room, I am reminded of that moment with Zlatá under the spouting rain, among the creaking pines and naked maples, and the smell of an awakening earth. I look at Anežka and as her eyes squint with laughter, I see the echo of Zlatá. And in this fleeting moment I have stepped into the green shades of that wet forest, with Anežka in hand.

Rusalka's Folly

In my apartment I sit smoking, watching the steeples and towers of Prague. I have placed a disc on the turntable and now am absorbed by the sorrowful call of Rusalka, beckoning the moon to shine down on her, and make her love known to the Prince. I cannot help but think of Anežka, her Czech mother and Jewish father. I did not stay much longer after Édith Piaf's melody gave way to silence. The song finished and we laughed, and it seemed to me as though any conversation would pale in comparison, and reveal my projection of paradise on Anežka as false. So I thanked her and bid my goodbye. I stepped into the alleyway quite resigned that this would be the last time I would see her, and though the encounter had been more than I expected, it had been much less than I wanted, and I chastised myself for such incorrigible desire. I dawdled back to my apartment, half expecting to see the police waiting outside, but no one was there.

As I sit here now, Dvořak's opera soars through my bedroom and kitchen and out the window, and I too call out to the moon to send a message of understanding to Anežka. And so like a fool I rise and walk to the window and implore the moon and the city to let me stay here a little while longer. Let me stay here with Anežka. Rusalka's lamentations soar above mine and tug at my heart, and I know it is an idle request. That sooner rather than later, Rusalka and I shall both be condemned to the places where we know we belong. Outside, the city sprawls before me like hundreds of nights before this one. Life builds us up, and when we look down we see that we have no footing, that we have in fact built a temple of empty air. If we pause only for a moment, that temple will collapse and cause us to fall, to end our mad ascent. But what happens to us once we fall? Some will fall into the open arms of those who care for us, and some, who have none to catch them, will tumble onto the hard rock beneath. We are forced to look up, to pull our necks as the invisible empire climbs around us, using the air, using the space, to keep us away, to make us unworthy of all as our temple lays in shambles about us. Who stands beside us? Who holds us up? Is anyone standing in the darkness with me?

There is a growing urge within me to take my things and leave Czechoslovakia, but I suspect that I would be caught at the border. Besides, it strikes me that I am not really the leaving kind. To leave: there is a growing attraction about such a prospect, and yet it also seems incredibly tedious. To start a life all over again, without any history but the one you pack in your suitcase, without the drudgery of memories. To leave and begin anew, step into another world and start over. Momentarily it is a future that cries out to me and begs me to take it in hand. But to remain in Prague, with all its steeples and churches, its hovering saints and meandering alleys. To build a life here on the banks of the Vltavá, such is my wish. I look out onto the dark streets and watch the moonlight spill out and soak the maroon roofs. A breeze whips through the air and produces the scent of falling leaves and coming rain. It is the smell of a hundred evenings spent under a hundred moons. A dog barks in the distance and its echo rises above the city in soothing anonymity. Rusalka sends her melodic supplications to the moon, unaware of the unfortunate repercussions of such a request. And I think that this would be enough for a man to live. Almost.

—

THE PERPETUAL FEAR AND PARANOIA that continues to plague my daily life is in no way alleviated by the presence of Jitka Navritilová. Her every expression throbs with disdain. Each morning as I walk into the office she appraises me, assessing if my attire or dishevelled hair can in any way reveal whether, like her, I am a true member of the Party. Because ever since she first laid eyes on me, Jitka Navritilová has never believed that I was good Communist.

Today as I enter, however, she is not sneering at me, but sitting at her desk with her head in her hands, weeping. Curious as to what could touch this woman whose heart is as impenetrable as steel, I ask if she is all right. She looks at me with her red eyes and for the first time she does not glower. She drops her confession between gasps for air, telling me that someone from the police station called to say that at least one of the warrants that she sent out on Tuesday was wrong. The police had searched for a counter-revolutionary and found an old woman who swore at them and cursed them for so offending her son, a man who had given his life for the country to fight the fascists.

My heart stops beating.

Cold sweat breaks from my forehead.

My gut rises.

I am paralyzed.

It is over.

Somewhere in the distance I hear Jitka continue to speak. She says that they have compared the name on the warrant to the name on the list and that they correspond. She presumes sabotage and that the police will be investigating.

I cannot show my terror, and yet it fills me. I pray to the saints that Jitka's eyes be wet with tears so she cannot witness my panic. To hide my trembling body, I walk to her chair, each foot as heavy as a boulder, and wrap my arms around her. Her body is shaking also, but it is not from fear. It is the tremble of disappointment, that she has failed the Party and its advertised cause. I cradle her and as I do I cannot help but weep.

After Jitka is sufficiently comforted, I sit down at my desk and hold my head in my hands. I cannot move. Fear numbs my limbs. I can almost hear them coming up the stairs. But no one comes and I spend the day in terrified torment. I am full of regret. It pours from me. For all my words of grandeur, diatribes against the State, against oppression, against the prison of existence, all that I want is to be set back into the crowd of anonymous faces, to become like one of the buildings fading into the background. But I know that is impossible and I chastise myself. It is not I who has faulted, but the State. And though I will suffer the consequences, it is the men with power who have done wrong, not I. I have done what I could, and though I might have done more, I am no longer an agent of their power. I walk to the window and slide it open. An autumn breeze floods the room in a cool scent of vacating summer and it comforts me. It reminds me that there are things beyond all this. I smile and resolve to be at peace.

In the late afternoon, Jitka approaches my desk. I smile at her and she mimics the action pathetically, though her attempt is noteworthy and I know she has softened towards me. She holds out a new pile of empty warrants and a new list, a new set of names that must disappear. I wonder if any people will be left in Prague when the Russians leave. Jitka once again attempts to smile, but fails and so returns to her desk. Promptly she takes her coat and, bidding me farewell for the day, leaves the office. My eyes glance over the names and I think of completing the warrants. Writing down the correct names, the names of spouses and children, dates of birth, occupations, and offences. I can see myself placing the accurate warrants on Jitka's desk on my way out and returning to my old life. Sitting in my flat and watching the city below me, roaming the shores of the Vltavá, basking in the sun, visiting Maminka, sipping coffee on late afternoons, and making love to Anežka. The thought passes over me and with a weighty regret I take the new list and empty warrants and slide them under my shirt. I take my jacket and walk home. My sentence has been passed.

SENDING OUT THE FORGOTTEN

IN THE SOLITUDE OF MY APARTMENT I carefully package the lists and the pages inscribed with the hundreds of names and slide it into a large envelope. Once they are all neatly tucked in, I sit at my typewriter and insert a new sheet. My fingers jump up and down as they write out my name, followed by:

D.o.b: September 10,1934;
173 Prokopskă Street, Prague;
No children
No spouse
Justice Ministry Official
Engaged in counter-revolutionary activities.

And then, with remarkable ease, my warrant is complete. I pull the page from the typewriter and stare at it. "Engaged in counter-revolutionary activities"—I read this particular line and find myself quite inexplicably bursting into laughter. It is the laughter that only a prisoner can shout when they have read their pardon. It is the laughter of a man who discovers that goodness still lies within him. It is the laughter that comes when guns are pointed at our heads but truth lives in us. We laugh because the world is absurd, because we are flawed creations, and because the saints look down upon us and judge. My laughter fills the apartment and rises over the city. For a moment it drifts up to the saints that live above the walking throngs. My laughter looks down upon the world and sees where men are as small as ants, where walls are as malleable as sand dunes formed by the wind, where communists, capitalists, fascists and democrats are indistinguishable from one another. Here my laughter soars and grows to an echo that stretches from London, to Berlin, to Prague, to Moscow, to Washington. Here my laughter dances in the ears of the powerful. It sings to them the lullabies that their mothers sang to them as children and reminds them that they are human, and surrounded by a family of humanity. From my small flat, my laughter joins the chorus of countless men and women whose laughter is constant, whose laughter disarms the powerful and causes them to cry. From Washington to Moscow, the powerful will grasp their weapons and open their prisons to try to stop our laughter. But they cannot, because it fills the sky and echoes through eternity. It is the laughter of resistance. The laughter of freedom. The laughter of joy. The laughter of goodness.

My stomach aches from laughter but I read the line over and over again. "Engaged in counter-revolutionary activities." If what I am doing is counter-revolutionary, than living must be counter-revolutionary. And then the echoes of my laughter melt away and I stand alone in my apartment. I do not want to lose my life. I do not want to be arrested. Nor do I want to live under the oppressive rules of others. I sit down on the floor in silence and read the line once again, "Engaged in counter-revolutionary activities." What have I done that is so good that I can set my laughter among the saints? I am not a saint, and though my laughter for a moment ascended to them, it has fallen back down onto the city and into my trembling body where it once again lies buried under anxiety and fear.

I stand up and return to the typewriter. Taking a fresh sheet of paper I slide it into the machine and begin:

> **To whom it may concern:**
>
> **We are the disappeared, the intentionally forgotten. Know that**

we laughed and we laugh now. Perhaps we have disappeared, and perhaps no one will ever see this or read our names. But if you are reading this, know that you have not lived if you have not laughed. Laughed at the absurdity of the world. Laughed because you saw goodness and felt it. We have laughed and dreamt with the saints. We have dreamt of living.

I take the sheet, fold it, and begin to slide it into the envelope that contains the names of all the disappeared. But then I retrieve the note and, opening it once again, write with a dulling pencil: "Petr Ludek and Zdeňa Havlová." I slip the note into the package and seal the envelope.

Outside the streets are dark. Only a few people are out and I know I must hurry if I am to avoid suspicion. I would not be surprised if in the darkness the secret police are lurking, watching me, curious to know in what madness I now indulge. I pass through a number of dark alleys in haste, trying to shake off any ghostly operatives. I hurry toward the British Embassy, the envelope pressed tightly against my chest. I walk briskly through the streets, sure never to break into a run lest I draw attention to myself. My paranoia grows with each step as I near the Embassy. The laughter seems to have all but disappeared from me, and anxiety eats away at my resolve. I turn the corner to see the Union Jack billowing in the wind. It does not comfort me and I cannot imagine the package that now presses against my chest anywhere but with me. These names did not disappear because they wanted to leave their country. They disappeared because they wanted to stay, to realize their paradise in their home, to become saints in their own house. Our dreams are not dreams of the West, or of western capitalism. They are not a hope to replace one kind of state power with another; but to regain our own power and choose for ourselves. I think of the cemetery where lay the fallen soldiers of our land, and I think that the West has such cemeteries. Acres of land where rest the rotting corpses of men killed by the State. Is it so different? The mighty will always send the ruled to die. People do not give their past, present and future so that they may have the right to consume unabated, but rather to have the right to live. And so I turn away from the Union Jack and walk away as briskly as I came. As the British Embassy disappears among the streets and buildings, I feel relief that I did not toss these names over the wall to be found by some western bureaucrat and filed away as proof of our oppression and their liberty. Western nations will take our names and flaunt them as testaments of their superiority; they will wave them in front of those whose laughter they have stolen, and tell them to be grateful.

I walk further and further from the Embassy, the names clinging to my chest, and I can feel them release a collective sigh of relief. I return to my apartment building. It is late and there is no one on the streets. I look around, fear causing my knees to shake and my mind to jump from thought to thought. Fear eradicates my dedication. I begin an unsteady march to the bust of Lenin that sits in the middle of the courtyard. With my feet I tap the flat slabs surrounding the plinth from which the bust's pedestal rises and Lenin sits in all his bald-headed glory. One slab moves ever so slightly under the pressure of my feet and I fall on my knees, my fingers prying at its edge to lift it. I have broken into a cold sweat and my eyes dart from left to right in a search for any eyes hiding in the shadows. I manage to shift the stone slab from its set place in the patterned courtyard, and it falls to the side with a thud that echoes throughout the square. A moment, and then silence looms once again. All I can hear is the sound of the sleeping city, the droning urban hum. I look at the small square of exposed dirt and gravel that had lain hidden under the slab. I pull out the envelope and then realize I cannot bury it like this. I return the package to my chest and slide the slab back to its designated spot in the stone patchwork of the courtyard. I brush the dust from my pants and overcoat, make my way to my building and enter as quietly as possible for fear of having aroused the curious ears of Mrs. Vrbecová.

Once in my flat, I launch a frantic search for a box or container that will serve as tabernacle to these names desecrated by the State. Deep in my closet I find the tin box that contains the photographs and souvenirs of my youth. With little hesitation I dump the memories onto my bed and take the envelope from my chest. It fits in the tin box with room to spare. Without contemplation or reservation I have replaced the memories of my past that now lie carelessly exposed on my bed with the names; this which has become most precious to me. Before I leave, I scrounge my cupboard for an old trowel that I long ago used to plant potted tomatoes on my windowsill. Briefly the memory flashes before me and I think it funny that I should think of that moment now, of all times. I find the trowel and tiptoe once again down the five flights of stairs. There is not a whisper of sound in the building, and its absence heightens the rhythm of my heart and lungs. I carefully close the door behind me, pausing a moment as the rusty hinges squeak. Then I run to the bust of Lenin and once again pry at the slab and manage to lift it again, though this time it seems much heavier. The dirt and gravel are revealed and I frantically begin to dig with the trowel. I try to make a burrow wide and deep enough for the tin box. The dirt is hard and compressed from decades of being flattened beneath stone. I finally manage to make a hole deep enough to slide the box in safely. It is not very deep but I must be quick, for my adrenaline has given way to fear. My knees shake and my hands tremble as I place the tin container in the hole. I am an incendiary mix of anxiety and joy, fear and excitement. I cover the box in a thin layer of dirt and compress it tightly with my hands. It is an unceremonious burial for those who will soon disappear. It is my own burial, but I have no time to stand and pray, to eulogize, or to make amends. I fill my coat pockets with the dirt that remains piled beside the exposed earth. Then, sliding the slab back over the square, I take a moment to ensure that it is not discernable from the others. I pat Lenin on the head and walk back across the courtyard to my building. I feel as though I have been relieved of a great weight, and yet now that it is finished I feel an incredible exhaustion.

Once inside my flat I breathe deeply. All I hear is the blood flowing through my eardrums in an unremitting hum. My legs shake, my hands tremble and I feel sick with fear. As I take the dirt from my pockets and flush it down the toilet I cannot help but smile. Tonight I am living with the saints and looking down. I cannot discern who is a communist, capitalist, fascist or democrat. I cannot see walls, only streaks of sand. And I laugh.

The Fates Act Cruelly

A long time ago, not long after I had graduated from law school, a friend and I were imprudently discussing the prospects of the soul after death. It was an intellectual debate brought on by too much beer. A third friend spotted us in the pub and joined us at the table. We continued our debate and soon the third friend became long-faced and sighed repetitively as he looked at his watch. Taking note of his displeasure we asked what was wrong. He groaned loudly and said it did not really matter if there was an afterlife or not, but that the prospect of oblivion was so terrifying and depressing, so why should we yield to discomfort when we could discuss more agreeable topics? (He also mentioned that the Party certainly would find such topics inappropriate and my friend and I bowed sheepishly to this.) I cannot help but think of this encounter now. It is not the fate of the soul that concerns me, but rather our friend's reaction to the discussion. Is questioning and debating so unpleasant as to be considered a sin? And what of today? Silence is the impenetrable shield that holds the State together. If Jitka were to ask: where are these people disappearing to, or what have these names really done? Or if the citizenry were to speak aloud of the illicit activities of the State? But to do so would invoke complicity and perhaps a sense of despair. And this is entirely disagreeable, so silence remains, and those who speak out are punished and made to be forgotten. For that is what we are: the forgotten. And while it is an enforced policy of the State, it would not be possible without the intentional blindness of the masses. But it is also a convenient policy, for to forget the disappeared is to forget the wrong of the system. To not question is to erase the unpleasant knowledge that complicity hovers over Prague, over Czech and Russian alike. Over us all.

There is no rush to the office this morning. I feel as though it may be the last day of my life, and so I lie in bed and watch the dawn break over the city. A pigeon lands on the windowsill and coos. I listen to the church bells ring out over the city, and I feel at peace. The names have been made safe, and even if no human eye will ever fall upon them again, they exist on those pages. We may disappear and be forgotten, but we will live on the page.

When I enter my office, there are two men waiting for me. My legs tremble but I am determined not to reveal myself and so I greet them with an extended hand and a pleasant voice. One is Czech, the other a Russian. They wear impeccably starched white-collared shirts with black blazers and ties. It looks as though they have been given new ensembles to impress a weary population. I invite them in. Jitka sits at her desk, peering into my office. With the greatest stoicism I can assume, I take off my coat and hat and hang them up. Then, much to Jitka's dismay, I close the door. Turning around, I tell them I heard of the mistake with the warrants. The Russian is surprised at my frankness, while the Czech stares at the plant that I have sitting on my windowsill. He asks me what I know. I tell him I know nothing except that I received a list of names and warrants and filled them out accordingly.

"Why did the police end up at the home of a dead man?" asks the Russian.

I want to say, isn't it better than a living man? But I simply shrug my shoulders. "I really don't know anything except that I received a list and then filled out the warrant."

"What do you think of me?" the Russian asks and I jump back at the strangeness of the question.

"You are my comrade; we both fight for the same cause." The words come from my lips, but I fear that he detects my deception.

"Tell me, what is this cause?"

"It is the benefit of the people." And as I say the words, my eyes darken and I cannot help but become sombre at the hypocrisy.

The Russian smiles at me. He knows I am not like him, and in my trembling lips he has found his perpetrator. How I wish to lash out at him, to denounce and argue with him. But I return his smile with my own, and he and the Czech turn to leave. As I say goodbye, the Russian looks at me and says, "I am sure we will see each other soon."

I respond with a pleasantry, and once they are out of my office I run to my desk and frantically begin to fill in the last of the warrants.

My fingers jump from letter to letter, and the typewriter rings as line after line on the warrant is completed. The typewriter comes to a halt and I pull out the first of many warrants that I will write this morning. It reads:

Bil'ak, Vasil
D.o.b: August 11, 1917 Krajná Bystrá
Prague
General Secretary, Communist Party of Slovakia
Member, Presidium of the Central Committee of the Communist Party of Czechoslovakia
Counter-revolutionary activities and traitor to the People.

Here is a name that governs our lives and causes us to disappear. As I pull the completed warrant and read it over again, I know that I may very well be staring at my own. But still I laugh. This man, as the principle agitator to Dubček's revolution, has condemned thousands to flee or disappear. For this, he and the other leaders of the Communist Party and the Presidium should be brought to justice and punished for the actions that they brought down upon an entire people. Liberty and the freedom to claim one's destiny is the impetus that drives me forward in this adolescent prank against power. In the midst of this, I think of the priest and I wonder if he has already been taken away, or if he still waits in the darkness of his church for wayward bureaucrats to wander in, searching for salvation. We make a choice. In moments of clarity we find some truth, and we use faith to bind them together, and then we choose. And this is why Bil'ak deserves this warrant. We always have a choice, and though there are some choices that should never have to be made, we must live with them and take responsibility for their outcome.

Believe me when I say that I have no delusions that some officer of the secret police will go to Bil'ak's home with this warrant and arrest him. Someone will find the warrant, and a frenzy will ensue to discover who in their midst has committed such blasphemy. I know this. I know this better than most. And without explanation, I sit here and fill out twenty-two more warrants for upper Party officials: Karel Hoffman, Antonin Kapek, Jan Fojtik, and all of the leaders of the Presidium. As I place Fojtik's warrant on the pile I place one more empty form into the typewriter, and just as last night I wrote my name and placed it into the envelope, so now my fingers once again type my own name, followed by:

D.o.b: September 10, 1934;
173 Prokopskă Street, Prague;
No children
No spouse
Justice Ministry Official
Engaged in counter-revolutionary activities.

I take this last sheet and place it in the middle of the pile, and gathering them up, walk across my office and open the door. I am glad that Jitka has already gone home for the day. Perhaps she will notice the names without even sending them off. Then all her suspicions about my counter-revolutionary tendencies will be confirmed. She will scowl that I should be so reprehensible a person (if person is even an attributable characteristic to so vile a subversive), and she will smile at her astuteness. I am glad that she is not here. I can take each weighted step, and bask in my parade to her desk. These are the last warrants that I will ever write. What I carry in my hand is the pinnacle of my career. It is a mockery of their system, their rules and ideas. I have taken the means by which they exact their oppression and given it back to them. This is my final penance, and so with a smile on my face and tears pouring down my cheeks I place the papers on Jitka's desk. Then I move back to my office and check if, in my enthusiasm, I have left any names behind. I have not and so I take my coat, put on my hat, step out onto the street and leave that terrible place forever.

As I WALK DOWN THE RAINY STREETS, my heart becomes so heavy with fear and sorrow that I am convinced I was coerced by some synthetic intoxication of fraternal zeal. That feeling is gone now, evaporated with the act, and I am left here empty and afraid. My faith is depleted. My clarity vanished. Who will sit with me as the police interrogate me, as they lock me into a cell, as they send me to prison, or worse? Who will take care of Maminka? Who will fetch Lady Zuza from the garbage chute? I want to weep. This life which I have so ardently professed meant so little to me, now seems to me most precious.

As I walk through the streets, I look at the faces that pass me by. They are oblivious to my torment but I feel as though they should pick me up on their shoulders and parade me through the streets cheering. And yet they walk by without a glance, without a word. With each step my feet become heavier, until I can no longer move and simply stand in the middle of the sidewalk, these anonymous faces passing by as the cool rain falls down onto the city. A sudden urge overwhelms me and I rush back to the office, weaving through the crowds of empty faces. I grab the door of the Justice Ministry building but it does not move. I buzz the buttons to the offices but there is no answer. And so I stand, in front of the door, with the rain falling over my face and I begin to cry.

A crying man on the street is avoided, as any plague might be. In the city, a man could die on the sidewalk and the people would step over him. Perhaps life necessitates such blindness, for if they saw, would action not be required? And yet indolence and apathy build walls around me, they build cell walls for all of us on the lists of names. But can I condemn? Can I condemn when I so recently wore my apathy with such blindness? I cannot answer. I have no desire to answer. I want to move, but cannot move. I want to run, but my feet are too heavy. I want to laugh as I did last night, but fear and regret keep my laughter at bay. So I stand in front of the doors, staring into the dark abyss that is my future. There are no hopes here, no fantasies, no revealing gardens of paradise, nothing enviable. I turn and walk, my feet become lighter and lighter and with tears in my eyes I begin to run.

I come to the river out of breath, legs tired. A miserable resolve has settled over me as I approach the pier. I cannot remember why I have thrown my life away, why I have given so much to be erased from this place. I will be forgotten. Here at the end of the pier I could throw myself into the Vltavá and let the water engulf me. Is there comfort in death? Will oblivion take me or will the saints come down from the sky and carry me away to live with them? My legs tremble and I feel as though I will be sick. My stomach churns and I fall onto my knees heaving over the pier and into the water. With each retch, it is as though poison is released from my body; the poison of fear, doubt, regret, all released into the flowing river. When my stomach is empty, I roll onto my back and look up to the sky.

Hope, guide me back into your fold and embrace me. Keep me pressed against your bosom and let me weep into your soul. Come find me in this place by the river. Look at this wretched creature under the sky. What have I become? What will I become? Isn't this what you wanted? Isn't this what you required of me? You have abandoned me. I have lost my life. I have lost the chance to make my life right. Oh great and wonderful God of children and angels. I am alone on this pier. I am alone.

Rain falls down on my face and there is quiet. I breathe. The feelings have subsided, the poisonous fear and anger and regret have receded. I do not doubt that they will return, but for now they simmer somewhere intangible.

I make my way through the rain, in no particular direction, simply to wander. Perhaps it is because I am frightened to return home or perhaps it is to say goodbye to this city that I have come to love and hate. As I roam, I think of the police waiting for me, so I take a sharp left down a street and wander into a courtyard. I look around at the familiar place and realize that I have walked myself to my mother's house.

The rain falls harder and stronger so I stand at Maminka's door and ring the bell. I hear her muffled voice on the other side of the door calling out, asking who it is. I yell back that it is me, and soon I am sitting in her kitchen, sipping a glass of brandy and wrapped in a warm blanket as she launches into a diatribe on why I should not walk in the rain such distances, let alone without an umbrella. As she speaks I see in her eyes a slow realization that something is terribly wrong, and she takes my hand and asks me what it is.

A creeping sense of shame grows over me, that I should have wandered here like a small child looking for comfort in his mother's arms after the schoolyard bullies have mocked him. At this thought I become indignant and only want to take my leave. Maminka becomes agitated and refuses to let me go. "Look, I've missed my favourite program," she says as she points to the television, where credits cover the screen. At this I jump up, and shout at her, calling her a peasant and a stupid old woman. My hands flail in fury as I mock her life, her selfish inconsequential concerns and primitive conversations. Her stupidities and my revulsion at having to placate her as if she were a small child. And as she buries her sobs in her hands, I realize that this is the last time I will ever see my mother. I fall on my knees and press my head in her lap. Maminka slaps my head, and I can only whisper my regret at having hurt her so. Then as we both weep she holds me tightly to her warm, wrinkled body.

Once our tears have subsided and we are both sitting at the table with glasses of brandy in our hands, I tell my mother that I did something and that the Party is after me. "You may not see me for a long time."

"Tell me, what have you done?"

I look at her, and she knows just as well as I that one must do very little to be taken away. And so I say nothing. I take a pencil from the table and write down my bank account information. "Maminko, take this. It isn't much, but it's something. You ought to go before they confiscate it."

"No." Her eyes well up. There is nothing she can say to alter this course, and so now she cries, now she yells at me, now she must accept the destiny fate has appointed her. I take her in my arms and hold her small body tightly to mine; trying to imprint this feeling of tenderness and love for eternity. And as she weeps I know there is nothing more I can do. There is nothing more but heartache, and so I kiss her one last time on the forehead and walk down the hall to the door.

Before I leave, I turn to her and see her leaning over the kitchen table. She does not cry, for her tears are all gone, she simply stares at the table, the way a mother must when such a destiny is appointed to her.

"Maminka," I call softly. She turns and looks at me, her lips quivering. Her eyes lost. "I am sorry. The world should have been better for you," I say. "I should have been better to you." I hope that she will run and take me into her arms and hold me as she did years ago when I limped home with a bruised knee. But she does not move. She stands there. I cannot bear to look at her any longer and so I turn and slip out into the hallway, closing the door behind me.

The Saints Take Pity

When I finally climb the steps to my apartment, I am exhausted and can think of nothing but my bed. It may be the last night of my existence, but I am too injured to care. The image of my mother bent over the table haunts me still, and I wish that I had not told her. But there is nothing I can do. No wish can be made, no formula created to solve such a problem and so I sit in my apartment in my wet clothes and stare out the window. Existence has tricked me. The butcher, Petr Ludek; all of them have fooled me, all of them ruined me. Even Anežka, a whore, has made me fall in love with her. What idiocy! What hilarity! How they must be laughing at their success! I curse them, and pray that I may be granted a soul that does not manifest its wrongs so astutely, propelling one toward destruction. But as I do, I reprimand myself for there is nothing to be done. Nothing. Only to wait.

I scrounge the cupboards for something to drink and find a bottle of rum at the back of my cupboard. I light a cigarette and sit at my kitchen table staring into the darkness outside my window as the rain hits the glass. I am still in my wet clothes; they are cold, but in their discomfort lies a comfort, a tangible expression of my torment. I drink and smoke until my throat is burning and my head is heavy.

My eyes close and my head falls to my chest, but a small tap at the window awakens me. It is louder than the rain and so I rise from the table, surprisingly sober, and walk to the window. To my astonishment, there floats the crying fat woman from the cinema! She taps the pane so that I should open it. Once I have done so she drifts into my kitchen and stands there in her bright yellow raincoat. She apologizes for the pool of water that drips onto my floor as she slides the coat from her shoulders. Still astounded, I do not know what to say. But she speaks.

"Well?"

I have no answer.

"Well?" she says again.

I shrug my shoulders.

"Where is the celebration?" she demands. "Where is everyone? Who else is coming? What drinks and food have been prepared?" She becomes frustrated at my silence and rolls up her sleeves to rummage through my cupboards. I am drawn away from the scene by a knock at the door. When I open it, there stands Anežka.

"What are you doing here?" I ask.

Her boisterous laugh clears away my anxiety. "I'm here for the celebration," she says. I barely have time to take her coat and tell her I am pleased to see her when there is another knock at the door. I turn and, opening it, find the priest standing on the other side. He is dressed in his black suit and white collar and he smiles at me proudly.

Having ceded to the prospect of a celebration, I say, "I'm very glad you could make it." He smiles and enters, saying he needs a drink to recuperate from the endless flights of stairs. I bring him in and while preparing his drink introduce him to Anežka, who has joined the fat lady in making preparations for the festivities. Just then there is another knock at the door and so I excuse myself and open it. Conversation and laughter fill the hall and cascade into my flat as I stand by the open door, my mouth agape. Led by the butcher and his German wife, there stands the hundreds of faces of Petr Ludek and Zdeňa Havlová. With their spouses, their children, and their pets, they occupy the hall, the staircase and spill out into the courtyard to the bust of Lenin. I express my surprise and welcome them all in. I am astonished that they fit into my small flat, but they all pour in with room to be spared. Hundreds of people. I know each and every one of them and, as I walk between them, with Anežka beside me, they pat my back and thank me. Some hug me, others kiss me on the cheek. But most of all they congratulate me, and when they do, I ask them why and then they laugh and slap my back even more.

Again there is a knock at the door. This time it is a more serious group of people and leading them is none other than Jitka Navratilová. To my bewilderment, behind her stand Kapek, Bil'ak, Svoboda, Husack, and the rest of the Presidium. In her hand Jitka holds a basket of wine and she extends it to me.

"For your friends," she says, smiling. I have never seen her smile so authentically and I invite her in, shaking Bil'ak's hand and Kapek's as they step through my doorway and into my small flat that now holds hundreds of people. They mingle with the others and soon we are all drinking and dancing and laughing. We laugh and no one asks who is a communist, who is a capitalist, who is a fascist, who is a democrat, who is a Christian, who is a Muslim, who is a pauper, who is rich, who is a Czech, who is a Slovak, who is a Russian or a German. As I dance with Anežka, we laugh and kiss and hold hands, but again I am drawn away by the sound of the door. This time when I open it, there is only one guest and as I see her, I take my mother into my arms and bring her into the room where the hundreds of people cheer for her and call out that they love her. I kiss her forehead, and hug her, and we all laugh. We cannot stop laughing. It echoes through the air and shakes the walls. Everyone from the fat woman at the cinema to Bil'ak, to Jitka, to the priest, to Anežka, to Maminka, to Petr Ludek; we hold hands, we dance and we laugh all night long. And as the sun rises over Prague we take our celebration into the streets, where our numbers multiply and we dance and we laugh. Here we are as brothers and sisters. Here we have, at long last, become kin.

I wake up and I am snug, naked in my bed. The window is open and a cool autumn breeze floats into the room. The bells ring and I laugh, not knowing why or how I came to my bed, and a strange contentment comes over me. My throat is heavy with cigarettes and my head is heavy from drinking, but my laughter soars out the window and down into the street.

I DECIDE THAT TODAY, as I wait for my arrest, I will take the train out to Orlický Hrad, the place where I grew up. I have not been back for over ten years because the place meant nothing to me. But now as a man who stares at his inevitable end, there seems to be no better place to go than the beginning.

As the train begins to move, I begin to feel remarkably sorry for myself. I feel as if I have thrown away my life for a cause that I never believed in, a cause I can barely remember. And as the platform disappears behind me, I quietly curse the name of Petr Ludek. I think of all the books I will never read, the poems I will never hear, the cigarettes I will never smoke, the beer that will not touch my lips, the food I will not taste, the love I will not feel. And yet what was my life before? Nothing but a string of declarations of indifference, while the State used my apathy to service their cause. My soul had disappeared; laughter, love, kindness, choice—these became foreign to me. Somehow I had been brought back to the world of the living; I had been resurrected by goodness, by Anežka, by Mrs. Vrbecová and Lady Zuza, by my mother, by myself, by the priest, by the butcher and his German wife, by Petr Ludek. My soul had been revived by this collective's faith in good, by this collective's hope. With the countryside rolling by, I regret all the things that I will never be able to do, read, or see. But I am grateful for such a lamentation; such is the feeling of a man who has lived.

In a little over an hour I am standing on the platform in Orlický Hrad. I am accosted by the memories brought on by the smell of the air. The soft autumn smell of the country; stoked woodstoves nestling houses in their warmth, yellow grass bending in the afternoon sun, sheep grazing in the roaming pastures of the hills that surround this quiet village. I walk down the main street. It has been ten years, but things look as they did. Only small things have changed: trees are bigger, some houses dirtier, others cleaner. I walk past a woman whose face I recollect, but her name eludes me. She looks so much older, her face wrinkled and her back hunched. She appraises me with the same look of familiarity, as if I am an apparition of the past. The two of us look each other over, each silent, each searching for a name, a moment, a relation, but none come to mind and so we do not stop.

I hop the cedar fence that hugs the field at St. Irena's Church. The steeple beams in the noon sun as a flock of sparrows rise from the field and conjure a swarm of sound and movement. I watch them fly in unison over the field to the tall trees that sit on the far side. Their chirp and song melt into an orchestra of sound, sight, and smell and I wonder how I could ever leave such a garden of paradise.

I walk the last stretch to the house where I grew up, taking note of the trees and sky, and of the creek bridge that had once collapsed in a spring rain. Someone has fortified it and it no longer sways back and forth when I walk over it. A tribute to progress, I suppose. At the last bend in the road I see a small boy. I say hello, but he does not reply. He turns and runs toward the house. As I follow him, I cannot take my eyes off the scene. It is as though I have stepped into a dream of childhood. I see my mother hanging the laundry as the late summer wind takes hold of the drying clothes and bright bed curtains, while in the distance, at the edge of the forest, I see my father chopping wood for the winter.

I am brought out of this dream when a tall blonde woman walks up to me, asking if I am lost. Behind her is the boy that I had seen on the path, and like a fool had mistaken for myself. I tell the woman that I am not lost, but only visiting the house that I had grown up in. At this she smiles and welcomes me inside. She describes to me the small changes they made to the house, how the plumbing was inadequate, how the windows allowed the cold to seep through, and how happy they have been here. The kitchen is much as I remember it and each corner is full with a thousand memories of a thousand days long ago, and I am left dumbstruck by the waves of nostalgia that come over me.

I ask her if I might see my old room upstairs, and she welcomes me to go up. I have to bow my head not to hit the ceiling, but it is much as I remember. My window still looks out onto the forest, where at night the moon would shine and sometimes deer would feed under its silver glow. The window catches the afternoon sun and sends a stream of light across the room, illuminating the floating particles of dust that float through the air. I sit down on the wooden floor and let the waves of feeling and memory wash over me. Those private memories that range from horror to joy, they cannot be expressed to an outsider without relaying every detail, and so I will spare you these memories that perhaps will not mean so much to you as they have to me, because I have lived them, and because I sit here at the end of my life.

After some time, I am drawn back to the kitchen by the aroma of cooking. I make my way down the stairs and know that if only fate would allow it, I could so easily step into the kitchen and see my beautiful mother standing at the counter, making lunch for my father and me. But the fates have no such power, and I return to the kitchen where the woman is making a soup. The aroma of parsley and sweet vegetables steams from the stove and wafts through the house. She turns and asks if things have changed much, and I do not know what to say. "Things have not changed, but I have changed, regretfully so."

She smiles at this answer as though she understands, and then asks if I would stay for lunch. In my eagerness to maintain this dream I accept without hesitation. I offer to help her and she hands me some carrots and a knife and I begin cutting. I am struck by the image of me, sitting at the table of my old home, chopping carrots; tomorrow my life as I have known it will be over, yesterday I was a subversive counter-revolutionary, the week before that I was a callous bureaucrat, and yet all along I was this—a boy sitting at his mother's table, chopping carrots. And I know Kapek and Bil'ak were once such boys as well, as was the butcher and Petr Ludek. And I wonder why it is that people so degenerate with age, become confusions of religion, politics, and selfishness.

I am introduced to the woman's husband and we all sit around the table in this kitchen where I grew up and eat a meal. They laugh and I laugh. They share their stories and I share mine, and my heart grows and is full of the joy that comes when you have arrived at a place after a long journey and know you are home.

As all dreams do, this one comes to an end, and I find myself waving goodbye to this family that has become my own; these that are to me the children of my past. As I cross the field I am filled with a contentment I have never felt before. I lie down in the yellowing grass and look up at the sky. A poplar looms overhead, its leaves clapping in the wind as its branches arch and sway. Above are the clouds that balloon and rise above the bowing trees and the rolling hills that melt into the crisp blue sky; there where the saints live and look down upon us. I stare up at the sky for a long time and I wonder if death is really the antithesis of life. What haven awaits us on the other side? Oblivion or paradise? About me flows a current of life. It sprouts from the earth beneath me into the yellowing grass, and up into the air where it is swept along by the breeze into the clapping trees and upward to the billowing clouds. Surely we are part of this living current. Surely we can tap into its perpetual roam. And shall I dare think of paradise as this earth? Can this truly be the Eden we banished ourselves from with our overwrought consciousness? The breeze breathes over me, bending the tall grass that surrounds me and sweeps on into the clapping poplars, soaring into the billowing white clouds and disappearing into blue sky.

I raise my head and look about me. All along the field stand swaying trees whose golden leaves slowly drift to the ground in spirals that dance along the wind. As I turn around and breathe in this glorious moment, my eyes fall on the ascending steeple of St. Irena's Church. I find I have an inescapable urge to enter and so I pull myself from my nest in the grass and walk across the field. I step inside the small church, the smell of wooden pews and stale air filling me with memories I had forgotten I had. But it was not a search for memories that drew me into this place, and as I sit down in a pew, the words come to me and I whisper them to the silence:

I confess to almighty God,
And to you, my brothers and sisters
That I have sinned through my own fault,
In my thoughts and in my words,
In what I have done,
And what I have failed to do.
And I ask blessed Mary ever virgin,
All the angels and saints,
And to you my brothers and sisters
To pray for me to the Lord our God.

I sit and say the words over again, not to grovel before a God that I do not know exists, but as a declaration of history. It is an evocation of responsibility. Again I whisper them to the silence and it is as though it is being marked on the walls. A record of my existence, imperfect and beautiful, flawed in its entirety. It is not to confess, but to remember. To tell the fates that I have acted independently from them, that I was not compelled by a system to sin, nor was I compelled to do right. A choice was made, and continues to be made. Here I am, spiritually stripped, declaring before God and the saints that I am, and have been, and will continue to be.

Uncaptured Regrets

I had spent so much time at my old home, in the field and in the church that I had to run from St. Irena's to the station, and then was barely in time to catch my train. On the platform in Prague, my heart is heavy from the beauty I have seen and have now lost forever. The images of the day will haunt and comfort me, cause me torment and hold my salvation. I look at the time and make way to the lounge to meet Anežka for what in all likelihood will be my last meal. I had asked her to meet me elsewhere, but she had asked why I couldn't come to the lounge, and I felt repugnance at the prospect. But still I find myself walking down the street in the direction of the lounge, rather than to my apartment, where the police may be waiting for me. I doubt that I will tell Anežka of my impending disappearance. Detailing how I have orchestrated my own doom would only serve to confirm the very facts that I am trying to overlook—that I have only a few hours left of this life. And so I will sit with her. We will eat, we will talk, we will make love, and I will live in a fantasy of an existing tomorrow.

Here on my last night on earth I sit, eating and drinking with Anežka, a woman who by any measure is a prostitute. Someone I have paid to be with me, dozens, perhaps a hundred times and yet I cannot take my eyes off her. Her lips, her hair, her breasts, her eyes, they thrill my senses. She looks at me curiously and smiles. If I did not think it beautiful I should feel embarrassed at our adolescent flirting and awkward conversation. There is an innocence to love that I did not know. One reverts to childhood and stands before their lover with their hands open, a stupid expression on their face: glorious and pathetic, sad and happy. As I sit before Anežka, these emotions fill my head and make me dizzy. Regret for having been so foolish, irritation for loving her now at the end of things, awe that I have found such a woman, joy that she looks into my eyes, anger that she will leave this place and sleep with men because they give her money, and passion. Passion for her, for all of her, joins these feelings as they assemble in my mind. I look at her, listen to her voice, her breathing. An urge to take her in my arms and make love to her takes hold of me. But I remain as I am, memorizing an image of her, to hide somewhere in the back of my mind where they will not find it.

Yet in all this, there exists a lamentation that grows as our conversation is crowded out by the inexcusable groaning and groping, of men grabbing these women and laughing with odious affectation. I think of Édith Piaf's ferocious declaration of life without regret and I wish that our surroundings would melt away and be replaced by the fantasy of Anežka's small flat. So I ask her if we can leave, if we can go back to her flat and have a drink and talk there. Straightforwardly she looks at me and says she'd prefer to stay here. And her polite refusal strikes me through. For Anežka, it is work to sit here with me. Perhaps easier work, fairer work than to sit with another, but work nonetheless. I ask her again to take me to her flat and she tells me she cannot. I turn to look at a conceited man sitting near us, who holds a young girl in his lap as if this moment were the pinnacle of her existence. I turn to Anežka and my eyes sink into hers. In the midst of my adolescent verve I missed the unfortunate circumstance of our encounter. That I am customer and she is product. What mournful indulgence of love have I wrought upon myself? What of Anežka? What of this place? I am compelled to ask how she found herself here, and so I do.

"Why do you need to know?"

"Please, you don't understand. I must know."

"I don't see why," she says indignantly.

"Please, let us step outside," I appeal, and she cannot deny my persistence. We walk down the hall where, behind closed doors, men are caught in fornication. Once I am gone, she will remain here, just as she did before. And I grieve that her life should be so unaffected by my presence, and by my departure, as though I have meant nothing. I think of my conceited proclamations in the church and I feel ashamed.

We step out the back door. It is cool outside, and a brisk wind blows down the alley, launching Anežka's hair into a dance. For a moment we stand in the wind, and I wish it would sweep us away from this place. But it does not, and as I look at Anežka, I want to scream out that I adore her. "I am different. You said so yourself," I say.

For a moment Anežka does not reply. "I am happy for you," she tells me at last and I see that my transformation has done nothing to affect her, nor should I have ever expected it to.

"Why do you do this? Why will you go back into that place and fuck a man because he paid for you?"

She looks into my eyes, her own burning with frustration. "Why does it matter to you so? If I told you I was here so that I can put bread on the table for a child? Or I was here because when I was a girl, men forced themselves on me, and now this is all I know? Or if I told you I was here simply as a choice of profession, just as you sit at a desk, so I lie on a bed? Because there are men like you, I do what I do." Her tone is resolute. "If I appealed to you for my rescue, I would be virtuous in your eyes. But if it is a choice that brings me here, will you condemn me as a whore? I will not tell you why I come here. I do not ask you why you come here or why you sit with me, and pay me to do what you cannot find elsewhere. I am what you know me to be, what I have said and done. Judge me by these things, and not for anything but this." She turns to step back inside.

I am tired of thinking and feeling, so I follow her. We make our way down the hall and I stop her as we reach her room. She opens the door and slips inside without a word. I follow her in, resigned to act out the moment I had imagined. She begins to undress, each inch of her flesh slowly revealed to me. It is a sight I have seen many times, and yet today it is different, contrived, made heavier with my implacable sorrow. I undress and as I do, I think of Petr Ludek and his Zdeňa and I know that I am not him, nor is Anežka Zdeňa. What I would give to retrieve the love that weeks ago I had so violently and callously made disappear. But there are some sins that cannot be washed away.

Afterward, I hold her for a long time and listen to her breath. It is a sound I do not want to forget. In the silence I whisper into her ear, "I love you Anežka," and as I do, I regret it. The words sound foolish.

She turns to me, holding my face with her hands. "I know."

Her brown eyes express a kind of pity, an aching amusement that she should have made a man such as me fall for her. She is grateful to me, perhaps even likes me, but she does not love me. I push her away and stand up. I walk over to where I had dropped my clothes and, with the embarrassment of a child, slide back into them. I cannot look at Anežka. She asks me to stay. She asks me to talk with her. But embarrassment, regret, shame, the anguish of rejection; this is not the way in which I had intended on ending my life.

"Please don't leave." She pauses but I make no reply, and in her breaking voice I can hear the sound of held-back tears. "Remember that moment in my flat?"

"Our lives are full of regret, Anežka. You are a whore, and I am a stupid pathetic man." I walk to the dresser and lay out all the money I have left in my pockets, then I step into the hallway and close the door behind me.

I SIT IN THE DARKNESS OF MY FLAT. The street lamps have grown bright, and their light filters through the curtain and falls on my ceiling, creating worlds of shapes and form. I know they will be here for me soon, for I could see their black cars at the far end of the street, watching my pathetic march up Prokopskă and past the bust of Lenin. Yet I can only think of Anežka, and I know that I spoke wrongly, that I allowed rage to conquer my reason and affection. I long for one last encounter with her, to kneel before her and beg for forgiveness. But all that is done now. There is nothing else I can do; no words can be spoken, no wrong made right. Yet for all this, part of me must be grateful, for I know I am a better man for having known her.

A cool October breeze passes through the curtain, sending it to float on its invisible waves. It hovers on the wind, as if it were trying to follow the flow of the breeze, beckoning to be taken away, to fly over the earth and see all its majesty, all its suffering glory. But I know that even if the curtain were able to stay with the wind, to be carried away and fly, it would fall. It will fall because it was made by us, and it can rise to the occasion, reach the heights of God, but it will be only for a moment, for it will tumble back down to the earth. The breeze hits my face and the same yearning to fly upon the crest of the wind fills me. To float away on the wind. Away from Prague. Away from Anežka. Away from communists or capitalists, away from fascists and republicans, away from the world of men. The breeze passes over my skin, and my soul cries out to it. For here I will stay. Here I will carry the sin of Adam. Here we will live in this treacherous garden of men. And the breeze ceases and the curtain falls to the window ledge.

The soft putter of cars pulling up in front of my building sends my stomach in twists. The slam of car doors rings in my ears. It is like the sound of a whip snapping against my flesh. Tears fill my eyes and fear floods my brain. I know they are here to take me away. They are here to make me disappear. I try to stand but my legs give out and I fall on the floor. Sweat pours from me and my arms and hands are shaking. I crawl across the floor to the washroom, but I hear Mrs. Vrbecová opening the door and the sounds of words I cannot decipher. In this spinning world, my stomach seizes and I vomit on the floor in front of me. This is not the way that Petr Ludek went. There is no glory in this. There is nothing dignified about the State coming to take a man away. There is nothing formidable about being the man that is made to disappear. I will be made to be forgotten. And those names. The names on those lists. Warrants have been issued for them again, and if they are not sitting in a jail at the moment, they soon will be. So now, as my mouth is filled with the acid of my stomach, I must ask; what have I done? What will history make of me? None will remember and I will disappear.

I can hear the men making their way up the stairs. I can hear their feet stomping from one step to the next. Each sound marks my end. I lie on the floor amid the contents of my stomach and cannot move. Yet through this chorus breaks a gentle sound and I look to the window. The curtain is billowing, floating along with the wind. The breeze enters my apartment and touches my face. A cool tender kiss, quietly caressing my skin. I see the curtain billow, I feel the wind on my face and I can breathe. I see the world again. I turn around and look up to the ceiling, where worlds of shape and form flicker in endless patterns of light and shadow. To navigate this world, with all its darkness and its light, to find our way through the endless expanse of grey, to whisper to the saints that we have touched goodness, felt it, believed it, and claimed it, to know that for a moment, we have claimed righteousness; this is what life is for.

I can hear them coming, they are almost at the door. I rise to my trembling feet. My legs stay steady. I walk to the kitchen and wash my mouth and face. I turn around; the wind is still blowing through my window. I walk up to it and let the cooling wind wash away my sins. I think of the names, the lists, the warrants and then I hear the footsteps stop and a heavy knocking at my door. I walk up to it and open it. The Russian and the Czech, with four others, are standing there, dressed in heavy coats and black fedoras.

They tell me they are here to arrest me.

I turn and take my coat and hat.

I step into the hallway, flanked by the Russian and the Czech, while the other four enter my apartment. I only stumble once as I walk down the stairs. As I step into the street, I feel the wind hit my face. Along either side of me, standing at attention, are Petr Ludek and Zdeňa Havlová, the butcher and his German wife, the student and the priest, Ludmilla Drahoslavová and her child; all of them. Each and every name that has been etched into my memory. Here they stand as I make my procession. And when I stumble, it is they who gently bid me to rise.

The officer slams the car door and I look out at the faces. Some wave, some weep, some raise their fist in defiance. And when the car begins to drive off I cannot help but laugh, because at long last, I have found goodness.

ACKNOWLEDGEMENTS

I would like to thank everyone at 3-Day Books and Arsenal Pulp Press, especially Melissa Edwards, whose patience and guidance throughout this process was always a great comfort. Your support in this endeavour was indomitable.

I would like to thank my brother, without whose support I never would have written a word or committed to the 3-Day Novel Contest, and my sister, whose cupcakes sustained me during the marathon, and whose dedication to this work in these last few months has outdone my own. I thank you, and owe you both more than you know.

But this story could not have been written without the impossible choice of my mother and her parents to stand up against injustice when there was so little hope of success. I hope that I have in a small way shone some light upon the courage that through your lives moves us into action.

ABOUT THE AUTHOR

photo: Jakob Kupferschmidt

John Kupferschmidt took his inspiration for this book from the experience of his parents, who came to Canada as refugees from the former Yugoslavia and the former Czechoslovakia. John studied International Development at McGill University, during which time he also worked at the Canadian Human Rights Commission in both Ottawa and Montreal. He has worked in housing and relief projects in Africa and was a founding member of the Habitat Canada National Youth Council. He now lives and writes in Ottawa, Ontario.

ABOUT THE INTERNATIONAL 3-DAY NOVEL CONTEST

The 3-Day Novel Contest is a literary tradition that began in a Vancouver pub in 1977, when a handful of restless writers, invoking the spirit of Kerouac, dared each other to go home and write an entire novel over the weekend. A tradition was born and today, every Labour Day Weekend, hundreds of writers from all over the world take up this notorious challenge. In the three decades since its birth, the contest has become its own literary genre and has produced dozens of published novels, thousands of unique first drafts, and countless great ideas.

The International 3-Day Novel Contest is now an independent organization, managed by a dedicated team of volunteers in Vancouver and Toronto, but it owes its existence to the publishing houses that began and sustained it, including Arsenal Pulp Press, Anvil Press and Blue Lake Books. We at the contest also thank *Geist* magazine, for its continued support, and BookTelevision, for adding a new element to the tradition with its 3-Day Novel Contest reality TV series, which launched in 2006. We are also in great debt to our volunteer judges, who give hours and hours to reading and evaluating the hundreds of novels that arrive after Labour Day each year.

For information on entering the 3-Day Novel Contest, and for a list of other winning novels published by the contest, visit us at www.3daynovel.com.